Someone's Trapped

VIKING CLUB MYSTERY NO. 2

Written and Illustrated
by Maureen Grenier

*To Griff
I wish you joy in reading!
Maureen Grenier*

Copyright © 2014 by Maureen Grenier
First Edition — January 2014

ISBN
978-1-4602-3477-8 (Hardcover)
978-1-4602-3478-5 (Paperback)
978-1-4602-3479-2 (eBook)

All rights reserved.

All names, characters, and events in this story are entirely fictitious. This book is protected by United States and Canadian copyright law and may not be reproduced, distributed, transmitted, displayed, published or broadcast without the prior written permission of the author.

Produced by:

FriesenPress

Suite 300 — 852 Fort Street
Victoria, BC, Canada V8W 1H8

www.friesenpress.com

Distributed to the trade by The Ingram Book Company

Dedicated With Love
To My Children
Berni, Renée, and Chris

VIKING CLUB MYSTERIES

Something's Missing

Someone's Trapped

Table of Contents

ACKNOWLEDGMENTS	vii
PROLOGUE	viii
CHAPTER ONE – Out Of The Play	1
CHAPTER TWO – Trouble, Trouble	10
CHAPTER THREE – A Surprising Discovery	20
CHAPTER FOUR – Using Your Head	30
CHAPTER FIVE – A Steal	36
CHAPTER SIX – Winning The Race	47
CHAPTER SEVEN – A Good Tip	53
CHAPTER EIGHT – The Summons	60
CHAPTER NINE – A Blistering Memory	69
CHAPTER TEN – Too Many Suspects	76
CHAPTER ELEVEN – Plans Unfold	87
CHAPTER TWELVE – Locked And Loaded	92
CHAPTER THIRTEEN – Trapped	99
CHAPTER FOURTEEN – Showdown	105
CHAPTER FIFTEEN – The Viking Club Agency Scores Again	111
ABOUT THE AUTHOR	119

ACKNOWLEDGMENTS

I'm very grateful to all the people who have helped me bring *Someone's Trapped* to life. In particular, thanks to my daughter Renée who kindly reads everything I write — even the ghastly first drafts — proofs, edits, and helps name characters and locations when I'm stuck.

Many thanks to Corry-Ann Ardell, my good friend since high school days and a writer, too, who proofed *Someone's Trapped* and offered editing advice, as well.

And to my wonderful soccer-playing grandchildren Rebecca and Blair, thank you for being my soccer consultants, and for proofing the book, too. You're both awesome.

PROLOGUE

The dressing room is empty. The chatter of waiting parents and the noise of the players practicing on the soccer field filter through from outside, punctuated by the occasional piercing shriek of the coach's whistle.

The door opens and a silent figure slips inside. Swift fingers begin searching, confidently, carefully, and then pause. Here it is. A deep breath. No one can see. Can they? A quick glance around. No. The door opens again and shuts quietly. The room is empty once more.

CHAPTER ONE

OUT OF THE PLAY

"Hey, Todd! Todd!" Chris shouted desperately as he raced towards the Raider's net, but Todd ignored him and continued dribbling the soccer ball up the field toward the goal, running hard, two defenders closing in on him. The goalie was just inside the 18-yard box, facing Todd, crouched, ready for the ball, leaving Chris only green grass ahead and a clear expanse of net. But there was no pass from Todd. Instead, one of the opposing team players from the Raiders moved in, used his elbow to bump Todd off balance without being seen by the referee, and kicked the soccer ball out from under him.

Chris turned with everyone else as the play moved back up the field towards the Viking's net, the ball now in the Raider's possession.

The coach called to Todd from the sidelines, "Good try, Todd! Watch for a chance to pass when you're caught!"

Good try? Chris thought bitterly to himself. Todd had been well aware he was going to be nailed by the Raider defender and that Chris was free; he just wasn't going to pass to him, end of story.

That's the way it had been since the start of the game. That's the way it had been since Chris joined the team. None of his teammates passed to him.

Sometimes Chris wondered if the coach even realized what was happening out on the field. I mean, really. How could he not notice? And what was wrong with the assistant coach, Mr. Eastwood? He seemed incapable of taking his eyes off Thomas, his own son, hoping the kid would, by some miracle, not trip over his feet, not pass the ball directly to an opposing player, and not score on his own net. Of course, if the assistant coach had any real understanding of soccer, or an understanding of his son, he wouldn't be the assistant coach and Thomas wouldn't be on the team.

The play turned again and now everyone was running up the field towards the Raider's net and the Raider defenders were spreading out over the field to try and stop the play. Chris outpaced his mark and tried to position himself to intercept the ball. It was really his only chance to make contact since no one would pass to him. If he could block a pass with his chest, he would 'trap' the ball the way he had been taught by hunching his shoulders forward and directing the ball down to the ground at his feet. Trapping wasn't that hard to do and he would then be able to control the ball, move it up the up field, and have a chance to score.

The play turned again and now Thomas was dribbling the ball up the field and trying to hang on to it, but he didn't have a chance. As usual, the opposition moved in, and Thomas didn't know what to do. A Raider kicked the ball away from him and passed it to one of his forwards and everyone turned and headed back in the other direction.

"Thomas, use your skills, use your skills," the assistant coach yelled, when it was too late for Thomas to do anything but chase up the field after the ball like everyone else.

Chris felt sorry for Thomas. That's the way it was for boys whose fathers needed their sons to succeed at some sport, and Chris understood that. Thomas didn't belong on the team and that's why his father volunteered to be the assistant coach. It was kind of a free pass for the year or, in fact, maybe for a couple of years — until Thomas got old enough to refuse to cooperate and he stopped playing altogether.

Thomas's real talent wasn't on the field anyway; it was playing video games. Chris had seen him holding court on one of the computers at school almost every lunch hour. They went to the same school but had never spoken.

Thomas was a grade ahead and never played sports at lunch hour like Chris did. Everyone knew Thomas was brilliant at video games. On the soccer field and in other sports, however, he was an outsider and he knew it and so did everyone else — except his dad, apparently. Thomas was one of the younger players on this team, except for Chris, of course, who was the youngest.

Chris's dad had explained the situation to him a couple of years ago when the same thing was happening to a player on his hockey team, and Chris marveled at the terrible things the boy's father would yell at him.

"Some dads are like that," Chris's father explained. "They give their sons an opportunity to succeed at some sport that they never had a chance to play when they were young, for one reason or another. They think if they do whatever is necessary to ensure a position for their son on the team, the boy will be the hero that his dad never had the chance to be."

"That doesn't seem fair," Chris said, very surprised. "I don't think Graham likes hockey and his dad must know that. Everyone else knows it. It's pretty hard to succeed at a sport you don't even want to play. And I don't know why the coach put Graham on our hockey team in the first place."

Chris's father shrugged. "I think your coach was desperate to find a manager for the team and Graham's father volunteered for the job. The boy gets to practice with the team; he gets ice time when we are up a couple of goals; and if he decides he likes the game and works hard, he'll improve, he'll get more ice time, and suddenly, everybody's happy. It could happen."

"In the meantime, he listens to awful things yelled at him by his dad, his game's not getting any better, and he probably hates hockey more than ever," Chris said with a surge of sympathy, and wondered if he would be able to stand it if he had a father like Graham's.

"He'll survive. There are worse things that can happen to a kid on a team."

At the time, Chris couldn't think of anything worse, but he knew better now. There really *were* worse things.

The Vikings players ran up and down the field and Chris ran with them as the play moved back and forth between the two teams, with everyone feeling the pressure and becoming increasingly tired, but with no one on either team able to score. The game was tied one to one when the whistle blew, signaling the first half of the game was over.

Hot, sweaty and feeling more discouraged than ever at the impossible position in which he found himself, Chris walked back to the players' bench at the side of the field. The team's towels and water bottles were strung along behind the bench and he searched out his and grabbed his bottle and took a long swig of water. He then poured a little over his head, shuddering slightly as some of it trickled down the back of his shirt. There was a slight breeze and it made the water dripping over his head and down his back feel even cooler.

"Hey, Chris!"

Chris looked up into the stands with its sprinkle of spectators, most of them parents, and found the source of the voice. It was Jaylon, a boy from his school who was a couple of years younger.

Chris grinned and raised his water bottle in salute. Jaylon's father was sitting beside him and Chris included him in his greeting. Jaylon's father smiled back and gave a wave. Chris met Jaylon last winter at a hockey tournament; he wondered if Jaylon was also playing soccer this summer. The two of them had actually solved a bit of a mystery at the tournament with the help of another hockey player who lived in his neighborhood, his friend Rebecca. The three of them had joked about forming a detective agency and solving other mysteries, but he hadn't really seen either of them since, except from a distance at school. Maybe he should call them all together to solve the mystery of how to get his teammates to pass him the ball.

"Your team is looking good out there!" Jayon's father called to him.

"Thanks!" Chris called back with a smile and then quickly turned away before any other comment might be required. He knew that anyone watching him closely would have seen that he had rarely touched the ball in the

Someone's Trapped

first half and it was downright embarrassing. He hoped Jaylon and his father hadn't been at the game very long.

Chris walked over to the crowd of players eating sliced oranges set out for half-time, and he reached into the big plastic container for a couple for himself, and then turned away as he sucked the cool juice out of them. He stared out at the field and avoided looking up at the stands again.

He was relieved that his mom had not been able to come to more than a couple of the games and didn't understand the rules of soccer very well. She always thought he played really well and was satisfied if he seemed happy, and he made sure he always created that impression. He didn't want to tell her what was going on or why. She had enough to worry about without wondering what, if anything, she should be doing as a parent to help him change the situation. He carefully wiped the orange juice from his hands on his shorts and turned back and threw the peels into the plastic bag.

He didn't want his mom to be upset on his behalf or to try and help. She had enough to worry about with his dad stationed in Afghanistan leaving her to look after his two little sisters and him by herself. Chris tried to help out with chores and babysitting the girls so that his mom could get out of the house by herself once in awhile, but he couldn't help out with Ella's nightmares that had started up recently. He knew his mom was really tired and he didn't want to bother her with problems she couldn't solve anyway. He would go on doing what he had been doing all month. He'd suck it up.

The whistle blew and Chris turned and headed out onto the field with his teammates. The second half had begun.

CHAPTER TWO

TROUBLE, TROUBLE

Rebecca stayed in the middle of the pack as she and her teammates ran around the perimeter of the field as part of the cool-down at the end of the practice. She was hot and tired, but felt good about the drills they had been running and Coach Lisa had twice singled her out for a compliment.

"Nice pass, Rebecca," she said, when Rebecca shot the ball ahead and it landed easily and softly right at the foot of the forward who was racing ahead and looking back at her for a pass. "That's the way to do it!"

Later in another drill when they were practicing shooting on net, the coach was calling out which corner she wanted each player to aim at and hit, and twice in a row the ball had landed perfectly where Rebecca aimed, and the coach had noticed.

"That's what I like to see, Rebecca," Lisa called enthusiastically. "If you can do that in a game, we'll win a few more."

Rebecca felt good, knowing that her soccer skills were improving. She had no illusions about her contribution to the team; she was a middle-of-the-pack player and not nearly as good at playing soccer as she was at hockey. However, she played only summer soccer rather than for three seasons every year as most of the girls on the team did and all of them played competitive soccer and this was a competitive international team. The only reason she could keep up with them was the fact that her tough hockey schedule kept her in top shape and, after all, a team sport was a team sport.

In hockey and soccer, everyone works together to move the ball or the puck ahead to the forwards or offence, who shoot for the net and try and score, and the defense or the defenders do their best to keep the opposing team from scoring on their net. It was the same principle in hockey and soccer, and she felt comfortable knowing the general pattern of the play.

"You know, Rebecca, you'll be starting high school in the fall," Mom mentioned the other night at dinner. "You're soon going to have to make a choice with these sports. You can't play them all indefinitely."

Maureen Grenier

"Why not?" Rebecca asked, astonished. "I can play summer soccer, without it interfering with hockey; and basketball and volleyball take place right after school; there's no conflict. I can do them all."

"You can right now," Mom smiled, "but sooner or later, things are going to change. You'll probably want to have a summer job in three years when you turn sixteen, and schoolwork in the higher grades will become more intense as you prepare for college or university. If you want to go on playing soccer, you will probably have to start playing on a team that plays three seasons. There will likely be conflicts between soccer and hockey, and you had better be prepared for the possibility."

"I can't give up hockey," Rebecca answered. "I'm so much better at it than I am at soccer, and it was so much fun playing with the All Star Team at the end of our last season."

She looked at her father, who was leaning over the table and carving up a piece of chicken on the plate of three-year-old Michael who was watching intently, dying to get his hands on the knife, no doubt.

"Don't you think I can do both, Dad? I would hate to give up soccer because I really like it, too, but I'm not as good at it, I know."

Dad sat back down after handing a spoon to her little brother, and took his time answering.

"You're not as good at soccer because you haven't been playing as long," he said finally, "but you've come a very long way in the short time you've played. You're on a competitive team and making a good contribution. You can play both sports again this year, but your mom is just reminding you that you have to consider the future, too."

"The future?"

"Yes," he replied. "It's getting more and more expensive to pay the fees for competitive sports the older you get; and the more competitive the team, the more demanding it is for you and for us."

"I'm talking about the time involved when I say 'demanding,'" he said, looking at her directly. "There is so much travel time and it's hard for us to get you to and from all your games and practices, even when taking turns with other parents. It's difficult with my shift work and your mom working and with Mikey being so young. I'm just saying that you'll have to decide in a couple of years."

"There were a number of out-of-town hockey tournaments this year and your coach said there will be more next year. That really adds to the cost, not to mention the equipment. Just the skates alone…, " Mom's voice trailed off.

"So, you want me to choose soccer over hockey?" Rebecca asked, trying not to sound too horrified, "because it's less expensive?"

"No, no, no," both her parents exclaimed in unison.

"You can choose either one," Dad said, reassuringly. "The reason we're even mentioning it is because you're such a good athlete, you could get a scholarship to university some day and there are a lot more soccer teams for girls than there are hockey teams."

"So, it's just something to think about. Something to keep in mind," Mom said.

"Yeah, we just brought the subject up because we thought you weren't working hard enough out there on the soccer field, and we wanted to inspire you to pour it on," Dad said with a grin.

Rebecca tried to smile back. Her dad was a big tease, always kidding everyone in the family and making them laugh, but she knew her parents were delivering an important message.

"I guess because I'm so much better at hockey and I've played with the same girls for so many years, and Marion is my best friend, and she...," Rebecca stumbled to a halt.

"I know," Mom said sympathetically, "you girls love playing on the same team and Marion doesn't play soccer. But she's away all summer at the cottage, and you still have a good time with the girls on the soccer team. Maybe you'll make another really good friend — not like Marion, of course," she added hastily, "but someone you can have a lot of fun with, too. You'll always see Marion at school and after school."

"You don't have to decide now; we're just suggesting you should give this some thought," Dad said. "Don't let it ruin your summer. I have so many chores for you to do around the house and yard here, I plan to ruin it for you all by myself."

Rebecca couldn't stop herself from laughing at that one. She loved the yard work — any excuse to be outside — and Dad had promised her that she could help him paint the shed this summer. She liked painting.

Just then, Michael managed to topple off his chair trying to grab a piece of chicken that was falling to the floor, and after the crying had stopped, the conversation moved on to other things.

Rebecca thought about that dinner conversation now as she was running the field with her soccer team around her. Could she really make the decision to play soccer rather than hockey? Without Marion on the team? On the other hand, soccer was a lot of fun, and she was getting better at it. She wouldn't want to give up soccer either.

"Okay, girls," called the assistant coach, Megan Milligan, clapping her hands, "that's fine. Practice is over. You did a great job and we'll see you all on Sunday afternoon."

The girls immediately slowed down and headed for their water bottles and backpacks scattered along the side of the field. The coach stood talking to the team manager and smiled and waved as the girls streamed past her.

"Finally the torture is over," said Janice, the tall, pretty, and popular captain, as she grabbed her bottle, uncapped it, and took a big swallow. "Let's go do something fun — like stare at the wall."

The other girls laughed, gathered up their backpacks and water bottles, and, chattering, turned towards the clubhouse.

The great thing about this soccer organization was that the teams had an equipment/dressing room all to themselves in the clubhouse when they practiced or played a home game, where they could change if they wanted or could store anything they brought with them safely under lock and key. Megan Milligan hurried on ahead to open the door.

Rebecca thought guiltily about the cost of her sports, which she had never considered before. This summer international team was particularly expensive because of the guest coaches, the international competition — which meant some games in the USA — and the occasional one-on-one coaching each of the girls received. That wasn't the case with the regular, year-round league, or the town house league.

Rebecca's dad had encouraged her to try out for the international team even though he knew it would cost more than a regular summer team, and he was very proud of her when she was chosen from the many girls who tried out. She found herself wondering if it was because he wanted to give her every advantage if she decided to choose soccer over hockey when the time came. She sighed.

"So," said a voice behind her, "is it really that bad?"

Rebecca turned and laughed. The girl who had spoken to her was new to the team this year and was already proving her value. She was a strong forward who had just moved to Canada from Mexico and her name was Genoveva. Her new teammates immediately shortened that to 'Gen.'

"No," said Rebecca, slowing down to walk beside her, "I'm just tired and hot, and I wish I could jump into a swimming pool right now."

"That would be great," said Gen enthusiastically. Her first language was Spanish and when she said 'that,' it came out as 'dat,' but aside from some pronunciation differences, her English was remarkably good for someone who was used to speaking another language.

"I have a pool," Janice turned her head and looked back at Rebecca. "Maybe you should come over some time."

"I'd love to," grinned Rebecca.

"Okay," said Janice, " we'll have to set something up."

They had reached the clubhouse and streamed in through the open door. A few of the girls left them to go straight to the parking lot where parents were waiting to pick them up. Rebecca, who had changed at the club, turned with the remaining girls to go down the hall to their dressing room and, as she did, she saw a boys' team straggling up the other corridor, and with them was her friend Chris.

Chris was in uniform and obviously a member of the team, which was surprising since they were under fourteen as of August first of that year, just as Rebecca's team was. Chris, however, was a year younger, and she realized he must have made the team of older boys, which meant he must be a really good soccer player. She hadn't seen him this summer although they lived quite close and she paused to give him a wave in case he looked up and saw her. But Chris kept his eyes down and didn't notice her, and so she turned and hurried down the hall after her teammates.

She arrived at the door just as Tiana was saying in a bewildered tone, "My phone is missing. It was right here in my bag; I know it was."

And that was the start of all the trouble that summer.

CHAPTER THREE

A SURPRISING DISCOVERY

Jaylon was feeling good. His soccer team had just won its third game in a row and this last win was against the team that had won the summer league last year and then went on to win the district championship. Maybe his team would be the winners this year, but if not, they were still doing well and the coaches were happy.

"That was a really good game, everyone," announced the coach, after the two teams, including the coaches and managers, had moved through the traditional lineup to shake hands and then returned to their home benches. The boys were tired but happy as they crowded around him, water bottles in hand.

"Now, don't let this win go to your heads. I happen to know two of their best players weren't out there today, and you can never be sure of what else might have been going on."

"You mean, we just got lucky today?" asked Terry.

Everyone laughed, including the coaches.

"Well, you really did play a good game, but there was some luck involved, too. In fact, there is often luck involved in wins and losses — sometimes good and sometimes bad," said Mr. Holt. "Today, we had some good luck."

"Yeah, like that lucky save Cameron made."

Again, everyone laughed and Cameron grinned and ducked his head. He had played well in goal and knew it.

"If you play well, you certainly deserve a bit of good luck," said Mr. Holt with a smile at Cameron. "Now, I'll see you all at practice on Wednesday night at seven-thirty. Don't be late, I have something special in mind."

"What is it?" asked Terry.

"Be on time Wednesday night and you'll find out," Mr. Holt answered.

"Probably some extra pushups."

"No, we have to run laps until everyone else arrives."

Laughing and talking, the boys headed to the sidelines to pick up their belongings and then, in a straggly line, followed behind Coach Hugh Holt and Peter Milne, the assistant coach, to the clubhouse and the dressing room assigned to their team.

Maureen Grenier

Jaylon liked the fact that they had a clubhouse and could safely store their belongings during games and practices. It was like the dressing room in an arena where his hockey team suited up and stored their hockey bags. Most soccer clubs didn't have a their own clubhouse. It was cool.

He hurried ahead to fall into step with Patrick. He and Patrick were summer friends — played on the same soccer team, hung out together before and after the practices, and had a lot of laughs. He played forward like Patrick and the coach paired them together many times last year and again this year. It was too bad they didn't go to the same school, but they ran into each other at different events around town and were always happy to see each other.

Jaylon had been nervous about trying to get a place on the summer soccer team when his family first moved to town at the beginning of last summer. He had already missed the formal tryouts, which took place in the spring, but his dad had quickly made arrangements for him to try out as a latecomer. The boys were friendly guys, especially Patrick, who helped him out in those first practices, telling him where to stand and where to go as the team ran through drills that Jaylon had never done before.

"I'm so glad that you'll have some friends even before you start school," Jaylon's dad had said enthusiastically, as they drove home after the first practice.

"If I make the team," Jaylon reminded him. "Do you think I will?"

"They have room for another player and they'd be crazy not to take you — you fit right in. At least, I think so."

They smiled at each other companionably.

Two practices later, the coach told him that he could play an exhibition game with the team, but it took two more practices and another game before Jaylon realized that he was actually on the team. He had tried to return his team shirt to their manager as he had after the first game, but the manager shook his head.

"Keep it. You'll need it for the next game," he told him.

Jaylon looked over at the coach who was busy talking to someone, and turned away clutching the shirt to his chest.

"I might have made the team," he said when he reached his dad who was watching from behind the fence. "The manager told me to keep the shirt for the next game."

"I suspected you had," said his father with a happy smile. "I think you might be one of the best players out there."

"Not as good as Patrick."

"No, not as good as Patrick, but almost as fast."

That night, an e-mail arrived from the coach formally welcoming Jaylon to the team. It was a big moment and mom told him he could have a piece of cake for his bedtime snack to celebrate. They *all* had a piece of cake to celebrate and it had been a nice start to the summer and to his new life in a new town.

Jaylon caught up with Patrick, who was captain again this year, and walked along beside him. Patrick hadn't played a good game and Jaylon knew it and realized that Patrick knew it, too. The coach had yelled at him a number of times during the game: "Come on, Patrick, pick up the pace!" and "Position, Patrick, position!"

The coach also mentioned between the halves that some players didn't seem to be concentrating as much as they should, and everyone knew he was talking about Patrick, who didn't seem to be doing anything as well as everyone expected. In fact, now that Jaylon thought about it, it occurred to him that Patrick hadn't played well in any of the games even though he was the team's top forward last year and had scored the most goals. He wondered if there were something wrong, but didn't want to ask.

"Did you see that big center-mid try to take out Reed?" he finally said. "Didn't even get carded."

"Yeah, I know," said Patrick. "I thought the ref would have caught that but I guess not. Or maybe he didn't want to."

They were at the clubhouse now, and Jaylon was following the other boys to the dressing room to pick up his jacket and change from his cleats to his runners, and it took a couple of seconds before he noticed that

Patrick wasn't with him. Instead, he was walking towards the entrance.

"See you, Patrick!" Jaylon called out to his retreating back.

"Yeah, see you," Patrick responded without looking around.

Jaylon paused for a minute watching. It almost looked as though his friend were limping. Maybe he was hurt, although he had shown no signs of it earlier. Some kids from another team were just coming through the door and Patrick seemed to be walking normally as he passed them. Jaylon gave a mental shrug and went on to the dressing room.

A few minutes later, he left the building and found his dad waiting for him, leaning up against their van chatting with one of the other fathers. There were lots of families milling around, parents, grandparents, brothers and sister, and players, too, going in and coming out of the building.

Some of the other parents called out to Jaylon as he passed them, "Good game, Jaylon"; "Well done, Jay."

His dad was smiling as Jaylon approached and opened the back door for him. "Nicely done, Son; I'm proud of you and your team. We all are."

"We all are," Mr. Miller echoed, stepping away from the van. His son, Tyler, who played half, also played hockey on Jaylon's team during the hockey season. "I guess I'd better go and find Tyler. Did you see him inside? What's he doing?"

"Just talking. He's coming," Jaylon said, as he threw his backpack into the van and put his cleats on the floor mat.

He climbed into the back seat and put his seatbelt on. It would be two more years before he could legally sit in the front seat, although if he hurried up and started growing more and got a little heavier, maybe he could sit in the front when he was eleven. Size counted almost as much as age. Meanwhile.... He sighed.

"I'll bet the coach was happy with the game," Dad said, after he finished his farewells and got in behind the wheel. He started up the car, and drove slowly out of the parking lot. There were always so many kids around — some of them toddlers — all the drivers had to be really careful.

"Yeah, he was. Although he wasn't happy with Patrick," Jaylon said. "Patrick didn't have a good game and didn't want to hang around afterwards either. Probably because he wasn't very happy."

"Yes, I saw him come out but didn't have a chance to talk to him," Dad said as he wheeled the car out of the lot into the traffic. "What's the matter with his feet?"

"His feet?" Jaylon said, surprised. "There's nothing wrong with his feet. At least, I don't think there's anything."

"Well, yes, something *is* wrong," said Dad. "I saw him hobbling, and quite badly, although I didn't see him limp in the game. Maybe something happened afterwards."

"I think I would have noticed," said Jaylon slowly, "but I saw him limping, too, just for a couple of minutes before he left the building. Then he seemed to be okay."

"Interesting, " said Dad. "I didn't notice any problem when he first came out of the building but, later, when I looked over at his dad's truck just before Patrick climbed into it, he was limping then. Maybe he didn't want anyone to notice."

"But you noticed."

"Yes, but he wouldn't have known I could see him at that point. Was there anyone around when you saw him limping?"

"No, and he stopped limping when some kids came through the door."

"Well, that's it then. He doesn't want anyone to know he's got a problem of some kind."

"Why not?"

Dad said, "I have no idea. But there must be a reason. Maybe it's nothing and the next time you see him he'll be fine."

"He isn't playing very well this season," Jaylon said thoughtfully. "Maybe there's something wrong with him."

"Don't worry, Jay," Dad said easily. "If it were anything serious, the coach would be told and he wouldn't be on Patrick's case. It can't be anything much. Just keep an eye on him when he isn't playing. Maybe that will tell you something."

"Okay," said Jaylon, worrying about his friend for a minute — and then he cheered up. They just won a game and the team was looking good. Patrick was probably fine.

CHAPTER FOUR

USING YOUR HEAD

"All right, that's enough practice on trapping; our next will be on heading the ball," announced Coach Jerry Cartwright at Chris's next team practice. The boys knew better than to groan out loud, but Chris knew everyone was groaning to himself just as he was. Headers were hard on the head and the neck, and it was the worse practice drill of all time — well, okay, except for pushups. Nothing was worse than pushups.

"Find yourself a partner and do five and then switch," said the coach, striding out onto the field kicking a ball ahead of him. "Line up along the center line with your partners about ten feet away from you."

The manager and assistant coach began throwing soccer balls onto the field and some of the boys scooped them up as they rolled near and the boys began breaking off into pairs and forming the two lines as they were told.

Chris secured a ball for himself and slowly joined the first line; he made no attempt to find a partner. He knew whoever was left without one would come over and, sure enough, he saw Thomas taking his time but walking in his direction. The boys on the team didn't really like partnering with Thomas much and no one would willingly choose him, but at least they didn't treat him with contempt as they did Chris.

Thomas was a year older but only a little taller than Chris. Chris had always been tall for his age and was shooting up past a lot of guys his age now. His mom had ruffled his short, dark hair the other night as she passed by him at the dinner table and said, "You're getting taller again. You'll soon be catching up to your father."

Chris hoped he would. His dad was six foot, two inches. Thomas's dad was not much taller than Thomas was right now.

Soccer balls rolled back and forth until every pair of boys had one for the drill. Chris didn't bother to speak to Thomas when the boy took his place in front of him, but gave him a nod, which Thomas returned before glancing away. Even though they went to the same school, they had never spoken to each other and had never spoken to each other since Chris joined the team either. Thomas would be going to high school in the fall along with most of the players on the team. The boys had been playing together for a few years, and were a tight-knit group, although Thomas had never really been part of that inner circle. He must have known he never would be either, unless he learned how to play a better game of soccer. But at least he wasn't hated like Chris was.

Once again, Chris wondered how the coaches could not have realized what was going to happen when they introduced him to his new teammates the way they did when he joined the team.

"I want you to meet Chris Canic," Coach Jerry had said to the boys gathered around at the second practice of the international team's summer season. "We were short a player and lucky enough to recruit Chris, who was the top player on his soccer team last year, and they won the playoffs."

Chris grinned stiffly and looked around at everyone, and they stared back at him. None of the boys spoke or smiled.

"I know you guys have been together a long time, which is exactly why we need some new blood. Chris is someone who really knows how to work out there, not only in the games but in the practices, too. He knows how to get the job done. He's a good hockey player, too, and you can all learn something from him about playing with heart."

"Yeah," said the assistant coach. "You'd better start working as hard as he does so that he doesn't show you up. Too many of you aren't putting enough effort into the practices. You won't win the games if you don't practice hard enough."

"That's right," agreed Coach Jerry. "We want to see a change in attitude at the practices."

Chris could feel his face burn. The coaches seemed to be nice guys, but they were killing him. How could they not know how the other kids — all of them older — would react to this kind of pep talk. The coaches might as well have told them Chris was a spy for the competition. His teammates would hate him and make his life miserable. And they did. They didn't care how well he played soccer; he was the coach's pet and he could make them look bad just by working hard. He knew what would happen and he should have walked off the field that very day. But he couldn't. He had already agreed to play for them, and he had to keep his word.

He stared at the coach who had ruined his summer soccer for him and tried to concentrate on what was happening today.

"Okay, you all know something about heading the ball but all of you can improve your technique," said Coach Jerry after the boys had formed the two lines for the header drill. "This is one of the most important skills you'll ever learn and about 20% of the goals in professional soccer come from headers."

The boys looked around at each other. Most of them had never scored a goal with a header, not even the strikers who had the best opportunity to score any kind of goal.

"You need to be able to pass and shoot the ball with a header when you are standing, diving, or jumping. Remember to keep your eyes open right up until you actually strike the ball. Use your forehead. You can flick the ball from the top of your head but we aren't practicing flicks right now. Use your foreheads. I want to see more headers in our next game."

The coach motioned one of the boys and stood in front of him. "To direct the ball down, hit the top half of the ball, and use the middle of the forehead for a direct power hit, which you will use for goal scoring." So saying, the coach threw the ball at Sean who jumped and headed the ball forward. It was a good, strong header.

"That's it," said the coach. "There's your demonstration. Now get to work. Five hits each and then switch."

Since Chris had the ball, he said to Thomas, "You ready?"

"Yeah," said Thomas and braced himself.

Each time Chris threw the ball, Thomas closed his eyes as it approached and Chris knew he was afraid of it. When Thomas made contact with the ball, there was no strength behind the hit and the ball just kind of trickled away in any old direction.

Chris made no comment and when it was his turn, he headed the ball downward each time so Thomas didn't have far to run to retrieve it. He was pretty good at heading the ball and knew it. He wished he could tell Thomas to keep his eyes open and that it would help, but he didn't dare.

The whole miserable business lasted about fifteen minutes, with Thomas's dad walking by at some point and saying in annoyance, "Come on, Thomas, put some force behind it," which didn't help at all. Thomas didn't know exactly when the ball was going to hit him because he couldn't see it with his eyes closed and was often making contact when the ball was on its downward path, which always resulted in a weak shot.

When the coach announced another drill, Chris was as relieved as Thomas probably was. They walked away from each other wordlessly. It suddenly occurred to Chris that as unpleasant as life on the team was for him, it was probably just as bad for Thomas — he was also having a rotten summer.

CHAPTER FIVE

A STEAL

Rebecca gave her blond hair a shake; it was almost dry. The bus wasn't here yet, and she was glad she wasn't going to be getting on the bus with dripping hair. She'd had a chance to dry it out a bit while she and Janice lay on lounge chairs on the patio after spending two glorious hours swimming and diving in the Marshall's pool.

What a life, Rebecca thought while she was lying there under the sun, and for one whole minute wished their family had a pool before she remembered Mikey. If they had a pool in their yard, she would have to watch Michael every minute while he played in and around the pool with some kind of life jacket on. That wouldn't be much fun for either of them. The little wading pool was a better choice for her family for now, at least, and Rebecca was glad to realize that she wouldn't swap Mikey for a swimming pool even if she had the choice. They didn't have an issue like that in the Marshall family; Janice was an only child.

"I hope the bus gets here soon," said Janice stepping out to the curb to get a better look up the street. "It must be late."

"No, I don't think so," said Rebecca looking at her watch. "It usually gets to the stop where I catch the bus about five minutes after the hour and the half hour. It must arrive at this stop about ten minutes earlier. So, it should be here in another minute or two if it's on time."

"Maybe," said Janice with a shrug and a sigh. "My hair is still wet — I look half-drowned. I'm thinking of getting it cut. Do you usually keep your hair that long?" she asked, looking over at Rebecca.

"Usually. I tie it back when I'm playing sports, but some of it always escapes from whatever I use. So, I look like I have short hair some of the time."

"If you cut it, it dries faster and you don't have to tie it back at all," said Janice. "Why don't we both cut our hair this summer?"

The bus approached and Rebecca reached into her purse for her bus pass. "I don't know," she said. This was the kind of decision she usually made with her mom, who didn't really care whether Rebecca wore her hair long or short, but liked to be consulted, of course. "Maybe. I'll have to think about it."

"We'll be at the same school for the first time when we start high school in the fall. With both of us having short, blond hair, and being the same height, people will probably think we're twins from a distance," Janice laughed over her shoulder. "Wouldn't that be fun?"

The bus had stopped in front of them and when the door opened, Janice quickly mounted the steps. Rebecca followed more slowly as she tried to think of how to answer the question. It felt good knowing that the captain of the soccer team liked her and wanted to be friends but, of course, she already had a best friend — she and Marion Barnette had been best friends since grade two, and Marion would be home at the end of the summer. Then she brightened. Marion and Janice would probably really like each other once they met and had a chance to be friends and the three of them could hang out together.

By the time they had found a seat together on the bus and were on their way, Janice had forgotten the question and began to talk about what she wanted to buy at the shopping center. The what-to-buy conversation occupied them for the rest of the twenty-minute trip.

It was fun trying on clothes with Janice, and she wasn't always looking at the most expensive items, either, which Rebecca thought might happen since Janice obviously had lots of money and actually had a prepaid credit card with her.

"Still got sixty-two dollars on this baby," she grinned waving the card at Rebecca when they were looking at purses; however, Janice couldn't find one she liked and so they moved on.

They both looked at bargain t-shirts and skirts and other neat things, and had lots to talk about just like Rebecca and Marion did. Janice and Marion would get along just fine at high school, Rebecca told herself, and it was good to have lots of friends.

The only sour note was that Janice refused to go into Rebecca's favorite store, Karma's, where Rebecca bought a lot of t-shirts, jeans, blouses, and other things as well. It was also the store to which her family gave her gift cards for her birthday and Christmas.

"Why don't you want to shop here?" Rebecca asked, very surprised, stopping at the doorway as Janice shook her head and walked on.

"What's wrong? Why don't you want to go in?" she asked as she hurried to catch up with her friend.

"Because I think their stuff is cheap," Janice said. "I bought some things there and took them back because they were falling apart after the first time I wore them. I asked for my money back and they weren't very happy about it. They treated me as though I had no right to ask for my money; I never want to go in there again."

"I don't blame you," said Rebecca sympathetically. "That must have been awful. Did your mom go with you?"

Janice hesitated, and then said, "No, she told me that if I wanted my money back I had to ask for it and learn how to stand up for myself."

"Wow," said Rebecca admiringly, "I would have died. I could never have done that," and tried to imagine her mom making her do such a thing all by herself. "You're a lot braver than I am. No wonder you don't want to shop there."

"You shouldn't either. It could happen to you," Janice said, motioning to the next store. "Let's go in here."

Obediently, Rebecca turned and followed Janice into the store, thinking back over the many things she had purchased from Karma's. Marion, too. They had both bought a lot of clothes at Karma's and neither of them had any problems with them. Maybe they had better be more careful in the future.

They finally stopped and ordered a soft drink at a stand in the mall and sat down at one of the little round tables. "This has been great," said Rebecca, "but I should go home soon. I have some chores to do before dinner and it's getting late."

"Yeah, we wasted time traveling by bus. I wish my mom could have driven us. We'd have gotten here so much faster."

"The bus was okay," said Rebecca, "and your mom made lunch for us. That saved us some time."

Janice laughed. "You're so funny."

Rebecca wasn't sure what she had said that sounded funny to Janice. "It's all been great and I love your pool. You're really lucky," said Rebecca looking at the girl across the table from her and trying not to feel envious. Janice was not only very pretty, she was a really good soccer player, and her family had lots of money. She mentioned that she was thinking about being a doctor, too, like her father, which must mean she had good grades at school as well.

Some people have everything going for them, Rebecca thought, and tried to stifle a sigh.

"I guess," said Janice, and after a short pause, "I want to go back to one of those stores before we leave. There was a t-shirt I liked and I might buy it. I just want to see it again, and then we can go and catch the bus home."

"Okay," Rebecca agreed.

As the girls made their way back to the store, Rebecca spied an outlet selling electronics, and suddenly remembered Tiana and her missing phone.

"What do you suppose happened to Tiana's missing phone?" she said. "Do you think someone took it?"

"Why would anyone bother? She probably just forgot where she left it," Janice said with a shrug.

"Yes, probably. Although Tiana seemed pretty sure she had brought it with her to the dressing room."

They had reached their destination and Janice didn't bother answering as they turned in at the store and made their way to the back and the t-shirt bins. However, the t-shirt wasn't in the bin where Janice thought it would be. "Someone's moved it. It's not here," she announced after a brief search.

"Yes it is; I found it," said Rebecca, who was also sifting through the t-shirts and pulled it out practically from under Janice's hand. She held up the t-shirt triumphantly.

Janice barely glanced at it, took it out of Rebecca's hand and dumped it back on the pile. "No, not that one. It was a different color. Why don't you try in that bin over there," she said, pointing to a bin that Rebecca couldn't see. "I'll keep looking here."

Rebecca walked over to where Janice was pointing and saw another bin on the other side of a rack of jeans.

"Oh, okay. What color were you looking for? I thought it was blue."

"No it's green." Janice bent over the bin and began systematically lifting the t-shirts that were all jumbled together.

Rebecca walked over to the other bin and could see they were a different style altogether. She moved a few aside and didn't see any green t-shirts at all. Maybe they were in the wrong store. She walked over to the rack of jeans and moved a few of them apart so that she could see Janice at the other bin and was about to call to her when she saw something that froze her words in her mouth. Janice was stuffing the blue t-shirt that Rebecca had shown her into her tote bag. Rebecca glanced up at the mirror that was supposed to discourage shoplifters and could see that Janice was out of its range. She let the jeans fall back into place and moved back to the bin where she had been standing. She felt as though someone had dashed icy cold water over her. She shivered.

"Hey," said Janice from behind her, "any luck?"

Rebecca didn't turn around, but shook her head.

Janice joined her at the bin and moved a few t-shirts aside.

"You know, I think we are probably in the wrong store," Janice said, after tossing a few items around. "I thought this was where I saw it, but I guess not."

"Let's forget it," she went on. "The bus will be here soon, and I know you have to get home. We can come back another day."

"Okay," said Rebecca, hoping that Janice would have an attack of conscience, pull the t-shirt out of her tote bag and pay for it before they left.

But Janice headed for the door with Rebecca following reluctantly and then falling into step with her outside the store. Had anyone seen? Would someone come running out after them and accuse Janice of shoplifting? Would people think that she, Rebecca, had something to do with the theft? She forced herself not to look back at the store, and tried to look interested as Janice launched into a long, involved story about how an aunt of hers never got along with her mom because her aunt made fun of her mom's boyfriend when they were young, and her mom never forgave her.

Maybe it was a funny story or maybe it was a sad one, but Rebecca had trouble following it. What was Janice thinking? Why would she steal a t-shirt if she had more than enough money to buy it? If she were caught shoplifting, she would be banned from the store, maybe even arrested and charged with stealing.

They caught the bus home and Janice continued to chatter away as though nothing had changed and everything was just the same but, to Rebecca, nothing was the same. She tried to respond normally, and to laugh as usual, but her mind kept racing over what happened and she wondered if she should have done anything to change things and, if so, what that could have been?

What if she had simply said to Janice, "I saw you take that t-shirt. You put it back or I'm going to report you."

Suppose Janice denied it and said that she didn't take anything. Rebecca couldn't prove she took it, and if she asked Janice to open her tote, Janice could just refuse. What if Janice told her she was crazy and just walked away and out of the store? The salesclerks were young girls who didn't look much older than she did. They couldn't do anything about it, and probably wouldn't want to know.

She began to wonder if that's why Janice didn't want to go to Karma's to look for clothes. Maybe she had been caught stealing and wasn't able to go to that store anymore!

And that's how things stood as Rebecca's bus stop drew near and she reached up and pulled the bell. She got to her feet and moved into the aisle.

"Thanks again for the swimming and the lunch," Rebecca said, smiling as though everything was fine even if it wasn't. "I'll see you at the next practice."

"Or even before?" said Janice.

"Not likely. I have some work to do for my dad for the next few days."

"Maybe he'll let you off for a swim."

"Maybe," Rebecca smiled, and she gave a little wave while thinking to herself, "Not on your life."

She got off the bus feeling relieved that the trip was over. Holy-help-yourself-to-a-t-shirt, Batman. My new friend is a thief, and I'm an accessory because I was with her.

Janice was not a good summer friend, she decided, as she walked the half-block to her house. And, no, she was not going to cut her hair. Look like Janice's twin? Forget it.

CHAPTER SIX

WINNING THE RACE

It was two days after the soccer game that Jaylon was in the park with his mom, his mom's friend, Mrs. Kennedy, and her little daughter, Sara, who was about two years old and very sweet. Jaylon liked little kids and wished he had a little brother or even a little sister.

His mom and her friend sat on the park bench beside the playground while Jaylon pushed Sara in a little swing designed for small children, deep and safe, with holes to put her little legs through. It was fun to watch that little smiley face framed with blond curls swinging towards him. When he pretended to grab her toes, she screamed with laughter.

"Would you believe it was only about eight years ago I was pushing Jaylon in a swing like that, and he actually looked something like Sara?" Jaylon's mom said to her friend. "He had curly blond hair, too."

"Mom," said Jaylon, horrified, looking over at her. "Did you keep my hair long like this when I was two?"

"Well, you had your first haircut the day before your second birthday, but just before we had it cut, you had pretty blond curls like Sara does."

"I sure don't now," Jaylon said with satisfaction, knowing his hair was just about as short as it could be, except for a spiky bit in front. "My hair isn't even blond anymore."

"No, it's not," his mom agreed with a sigh. "But I loved those curls."

It was a little later and they were walking down a path taking turns chasing after Sara who seemed determined to try and run off by herself as usual, when he saw his friend Patrick. Patrick was by himself near the pond tossing a ball up in the air from time to time and catching in it his glove while watching the ducks and the geese splash around.

"Mom, it's Patrick," said Jaylon urgently, as though he thought his friend might suddenly disappear.

His mom looked over at Patrick, recognized him from soccer and said, "Go along then. But Sheila and I want to leave soon because Sara will need her nap, and we won't come looking for you. When Patrick leaves, you come and find us at the playground again and if we aren't there, you go along home."

Jaylon took off running and his mom's voice followed him. "Don't hang around here in the park by yourself!"

"I won't," he called back over his shoulder as Patrick caught sight of him and waited, grinning, by the pond.

"Hey, what are you doing here?" Jaylon asked when he reached him.

"What's it to you?" Patrick answered with a smirk, tossing the ball up and catching it again before he went on with his explanation. "My Dad has a meeting with the groundskeeper and so he drove over and I came along for the ride." He nodded his head over at the white and green building not far from them, behind the tennis courts. All the park service equipment was kept in the building, and there was an office there as well.

"Good," said Jaylon. "I was here with my mom and her friend and her little kid. We live near here," he pointed, "walking distance."

"I remember," said Patrick. "Want to play some catch?"

"Sure, but I don't have a glove."

"That's okay," Patrick said. "Ten throws and then you can have the glove, and then ten more, and it's my turn again."

"Okay," agreed Jaylon. That's what he liked about Patrick; he was a good sport and fair. "Let's get away from the pond. I don't feel like going swimming today just because you can't throw straight."

"You mean because you can't catch anything," said Patrick, but he turned and the two of them walked a safe distance away from the water before starting their game.

"What's your dad seeing the groundskeeper about?" asked Jaylon after a bit.

"He might have some work for him."

"Oh," said Jaylon, not wanting to ask why Patrick's dad was looking for work. He thought Mr. MacLaren worked at the big plant at the edge of town, but he decided not to ask about it. "Maybe if he works around here you can come to the park again."

"Maybe," Patrick answered.

Just then, Jaylon threw a ball too high for his friend to catch and Patrick turned and raced after it.

"Sorry!" Jaylon called. He stood watching Patrick run and noticed that there was absolutely nothing wrong with the way his friend moved. There was no limp; there was no sign of any problem. Whatever the trouble might been, it was over, and Jaylon was relieved.

They went on with the game for about ten minutes and then Patrick, who was checking the white and green building from time to time, suddenly paused before he threw the ball, and said, "There's my dad. I have to go. He'll be looking for me." He looked back at Jaylon, who was using the glove.

"Oh," said Jaylon, "okay."

He walked over to Patrick and handed him the glove, and Patrick waved at his dad who was looking around for him.

Patrick's father caught sight of the two boys and acknowledged the wave with one of his own and then turned towards his red Ford truck, which Jaylon could see parked beside the building.

"Do you have the soccer team phone list?" Jaylon asked, walking along beside Patrick. "It has my phone number on it. If you are coming back to the park, you could call me and I can meet you here. There's lots of neat stuff to do."

"Okay, I'll ask," said Patrick. "I'll race you to the truck." And he paused, looking at Jaylon who also paused.

"One, two, three, go!" shouted Patrick and they took off together.

Patrick was always able to outrun Jaylon, but maybe not now, Jaylon thought as he poured it on. Patrick seemed to have slowed down this year, or maybe Jaylon had caught up and could outrun him now. He was certainly outrunning Pat on the soccer field this summer, but no, just as he thought that, Patrick pulled away, and Jaylon was at least four paces behind or maybe even more by the time they reached the truck.

Mr. MacLaren smiled down at the two laughing friends as he waited in the truck, motor running. "We have to get home, Patrick," he said, adding, "Nice to see you, Jaylon."

"Hi, Mr. MacLaren," Jaylon answered breathlessly.

Someone's Trapped

"Dad, will we be coming back to the park soon?" Patrick asked.

"Probably," his dad answered. "I'll know by the end of the week."

Patrick grinned at Jaylon and moved around to the passenger side of the truck. "I'll phone you if we are going to come," he called as he opened the door to the truck. "I know my mom has the soccer phone list; she keeps it in the file."

"Good," Jaylon called back, and he gave a little wave. "See ya."

Mr. MacLaren nodded at him and Patrick waved from inside the truck. Jaylon stood watching until the truck had moved on and disappeared down one of the roads that led to the street, and then hurried off to the playground. When he didn't find his mom, he headed home. He was glad there was nothing wrong with Pat — he could still outrun Jaylon easily. In fact, if Jaylon were ever going to beat Patrick, maybe he needed to practice running more often. That was probably a good idea. Maybe he should start right now, he thought and he broke into a run. He ran as fast as he could all the way home.

CHAPTER SEVEN

A GOOD TIP

Chris walked into the clubhouse carrying his backpack over his shoulder. He had come to the game by bus which he did more than half the time and didn't mind the easy trip. After dinner, his mom had again asked him if he could arrange a ride with one of the other boys.

"I'll be happy to take turns driving with a couple of the other parents," she told him after dinner as she handed him a new packet of bus tickets. "Why don't you ask one or two of the other boys if their parents would like some help with the driving? Seriously, you don't have to take the bus so often. I feel guilty about this."

"It's okay, Mom, it's really okay," he had responded. "I don't mind taking the bus at all. Some of the other guys take the bus, too; it's not weird or anything."

Actually, it was kind of weird, he supposed. There may be another boy who took the bus once in awhile if he happened to be on a direct route like Chris but, if so, Chris had never seen him; Chris had never seen any other member of the team come by bus or waiting at a bus stop. In fact, rather then have anyone see him getting off or on the bus, Chris used a bus stop a couple of blocks away to make sure no one realized he came to all the practices alone. His mom drove him to both of the games that weren't played on their home field, and the one time she couldn't manage it, he had asked the coach for a ride. How long he was going to be able to keep this up, he didn't know.

In the dressing room, he bent over his cleats and carefully tied up the laces and then pulled his practice jersey over his head. His teammates were laughing and talking all around him, and he very carefully didn't look at any of them. He wasn't going to make the mistake of saying 'Hi' or attempting to join in any of the conversations as he had in the past. Being deliberately snubbed was the worst feeling in the world.

He watched Thomas walk in with his father behind him.

"Hey, Todd, how's it going?" Thomas said, looking directly at Todd who was lacing up his cleats.

Todd, who had never passed the ball to Thomas and probably would run through gunfire rather than pass it to Chris, looked up briefly and said nothing. Then his eyes slid past Thomas to rest on Mr. Eastwood, Thomas's father. He looked back at Thomas who was now choosing a spot on the bench and his face relaxed into a big grin.

"Hey yourself, Thomas," Todd said loudly. "How you doing, man?"

Mr. Eastwood, who had paused to look at Todd when there was no response to his son's greeting, was apparently now satisfied that his son was 'one of the boys.' He turned away, dumping his backpack on the bench, and then stepped up to chalkboard and began looking for chalk along the ledge.

When had he ever found chalk on the ledge, Chris wondered as he watched the assistant coach turn away to get some chalk out of his backpack. Probably not since the Samurai warriors had suited up for a soccer game, which was, like, never.

Chris looked over at Todd who was now chatting with one of the boys who sat beside him in the dressing room. All the top players and the goalie had their own special spots, chosen informally at the beginning of the season, but remaining theirs until the season ended — or until a soccer player was carried out on a stretcher, never to return, Chris supposed. The boys in the lower ranks occasionally shifted places, but there wasn't very much movement among those boys either and, of course, Chris was one of them.

Thomas sat by himself as Chris did, but people did speak to him and they never said rude things to him on the field as they did to Chris. Thomas owed his protection to his father, of course. Chris didn't envy Thomas but wished he had a bodyguard, too.

The coach came in and picked up the chalk that was waiting for him on the blackboard ledge and called for attention. He then began his 'chalk talk,' telling the team about the skill sets they were going to work on today, diagramming on the board as he talked, and reminding them of things he was looking for in the drills.

There was no mention of the team they were going to play against in the next game; the coach always saved that for game day when he told them of weaknesses he had observed in the other team, which they could use to their advantage. Sometimes he would tell them to which side they should aim the ball when going in for a shot, or to kick it high or low, depending on where he thought the goalie was less strong.

He also gave them the numbers of the best players on the opposing team and which players he had assigned to man-mark them to be sure those top players didn't have an opportunity to get a shot away. Sometimes that worked and sometimes it didn't, but it was always an honor to be chosen for the job, the coach told them.

Chris seriously doubted the honor part because, if you were stuck guarding a player a lot better than you were, it was harder to get the ball and get away for a chance to score. That really sucked. Then he remembered that he had very little chance of scoring anyway unless someone passed him the ball. He might as well be man-marking Goliath in one game, Samson in the next, and Attila, the Hun, in the third.

The coach gave them a few more tips and then said, "Let's go," as he dropped the chalk on the ledge and moved away. Mr. Eastwood scooped it up to replace in his backpack and Chris wondered if the coach thought the chalk appeared on the ledge by some miracle each week whenever he needed it. He certainly didn't acknowledge Mr. Eastwood with a thank you, a nod, or a smile. Maybe placing chalk on blackboard ledges was a long-standing tradition carried on by armies of assistant coaches over the years.

Chris sighed. He really missed talking to his father, and he wished his buddy Blair played soccer as well as hockey and had been called to play with this team, too. He turned and threw his wallet, watch, shoes, socks, and cell phone into an empty locker, closed the door, and followed his teammates out into the sunshine.

After the warm-up was over, the coach called for the drill on heading the ball. He reminded them of what he told them at the last practice and in the chalk talk and waved them over to the pile of soccer balls.

Chris walked over and chose a ball, and then took a place on the line and waited. He hadn't counted to make sure there was an even number of players at the practice, but if there were, he knew what to expect — and, yes, here he comes. Thomas took his time walking over to stand opposite Chris, but the two boys were finally facing each other, both with a ball. Chris dropped his and waited. Thomas understood and lobbed the ball his way. Chris jumped and smartly hit the ball with the upper part of his forehead aiming at the ground a few feet in front of him. Good one!

Thomas moved forward as it was his job to collect the ball and throw it to Chris again, but Chris quickly moved out, picked up the ball and walked the remaining few paces to reach Thomas. He looked out at the field, and carefully not looking at Thomas, said, "If you watch the ball as it comes towards you, you can eventually time it just right so that you can jump into a position where the ball will hit the middle of your forehead. If you hit back at the moment it's hitting you, it doesn't hurt — at least, not like it does when it hits some other part of your head and you haven't moved against it."

Chris then turned on his heel and walked back to his position with the ball. Thomas said nothing.

Chris threw the ball at Thomas and watched as Thomas succeeded in keeping his eyes open, scrunching up his face as he did so. He jumped at the right moment, and drove the ball hard — not straight, but hard, at least.

Chris ran to get it, not able to suppress his feeling of triumph; however, he managed to erase any expression from his face as he turned and threw the ball back to Thomas. Thomas also showed no reaction as he headed the ball at Chris again, and the two of them lobbied back and forth with Thomas able to straighten out his header a little more with each volley.

When the drill was over, the boys separated without speaking, but Chris felt good, and he was sure Thomas did, too. With any kind of luck, Mr. Eastwood saw some of that and would ease up on Thomas.

At the end of the practice, when they were picking up their things in the locker room and Chris was tugging on his runners, Thomas walked by him and, without looking at him, muttered, "Thanks, man," and walked on.

Finally, thought Chris with satisfaction, I now have a semi-friend. Things are looking up.

CHAPTER EIGHT

THE SUMMONS

Rebecca was dreading the arrival of Sunday and the next practice. She had managed to avoid spending any time with Janice even though they talked briefly on the phone a couple of times, and Janice seemed to accept Rebecca's excuses for not being able to come over for a swim or to find time to do anything else. However, they would be face to face at the practice on Sunday and Rebecca was going to have to deal with the situation sooner or later.

She got out of the car on Sunday afternoon in front of the soccer clubhouse and tried to focus on her mom and respond normally when her mom wished her good luck in the practice and told her where to find the car after it was over.

"When I come to get you, I'll be parked in that lot over there," Mom said, pointing to the parking lot across the street, "so you will have to find me. I'll keep an eye out for you but, you know…."

"Yes, I know," said Rebecca smiling. "Don't worry, Mom, I'll find you. Bye."

She turned and started up the walkway, checking out the girls who were walking towards the building. She hoped Janice wasn't one of them, and saw with relief that Gen was coming towards her.

"Hi, Gen," Rebecca called, stopping to wait for her.

"Hey, Becs."

"Becs?" said Rebecca surprised, as Gen drew near. "No one has ever called me 'Becs' before."

"No one ever called me 'Gen' until I joined this team," said Gen. "Don't you like the name 'Becs'?"

"I don't care. It's okay," said Rebecca. "Don't you like the name 'Gen'?"

"I don't care. It's okay," said Gen, and both girls laughed. They turned and walked up to the clubhouse and through the open double doors.

"I saw Tiana yesterday," said Gen as they headed up the hall. "She still can't find her phone, and a lot of us were helping her look for it before we left after Wednesday's practice, as you know. Megan Milligan kept telling her she was probably mistaken about when she saw it last

Someone's Trapped   **61**

and probably left it in the car, or at home, or something, remember? Tiana said she knows she had it at the practice because she called home just before she left the dressing room, and she's sure someone stole it. She's not happy that Megan refused to believe her and insisted that she look for it at home."

"Well, Megan probably doesn't want to believe her," said Rebecca, who was no great fan of the assistant coach. "That's the easiest thing to do. On the other hand, how could anyone have stolen it? The door was locked."

"Yes," said Gen, "but someone could have found an extra key somewhere, or picked the lock, or had a copy of the key made."

"Just to steal a phone?" said Rebecca, pushing open the door to the dressing room.

"Well, no, probably not, but the summer has just started," said Gen seriously. "Maybe there's more to come."

"Well, I hope not," said Rebecca. "My mom would kill me if anything happened to my phone."

"If it comes to that, a lot of our lives are hanging by a slender thread. My mom would kill me, too," responded Gen.

"Are you talking about my sister's phone being stolen?" asked Matea. She was sitting across the room from Tiana who was talking to some of her friends. Gen and Rebecca took seats beside Matea.

"Yes, we are," said Rebecca. "So, it hasn't turned up anywhere?"

The age group for the international team was under fourteen, which meant that Matea and Tiana played on the same soccer team even though Matea was a year younger and a grade behind Tiana. They were both really good players and Matea was almost as good at the game as her older sister.

"No, it was stolen," Matea said. "She used it at the practice on Wednesday. My dad called the coach last night and suggested the clubhouse should do something about the security here."

"Sheesh," said Rebecca. "Maybe the coach will say something to us about it today." She pulled her practice t-shirt over her head and reached in her backpack for her cleats.

"Perhaps the door wasn't really locked. Maybe someone came back to use the restroom, tried our dressing room door, found it unlocked, and just came in and helped herself," said Gen, tying the laces on her cleats.

"If that's how it happened, it wouldn't necessarily be someone from our team," said Rebecca slowly, but thinking, of course, of Janice. "It could be someone from another team who tried all the dressing room doors and found ours open."

Had Janice returned to the clubhouse during the practice and got into the dressing room somehow? How awful. But if she stole a t-shirt from a store, maybe she'd

Someone's Trapped **63**

steal a phone from a friend. Could she really have done that? Where was she today? Almost everyone else was here. She barely finished that thought before the door opened and in walked Janice. Right behind her was Megan and the coach, Lisa Banting, on her heels.

Janice looked around the room, grinned at Rebecca, gave her a little wave, and took a seat beside Tori, who played defense, a girl Rebecca knew well because they had played hockey together. In fact, Tori was captain of their hockey team last season.

"Okay, girls" said Coach Lisa, "I'm sure you all know about Tiana's missing phone and we have to make sure nothing like that happens again. I'm sure none of you took her phone, but it's not enough for us to believe that; we have to be able to say that with certainty to the satisfaction of anyone who asks."

"How are we going to do that?" asked Tori.

"Well, we're going to have to ask you to report to Kim when you leave the field to use the restroom in the middle of a practice."

This comment was met with a wall of silence from the players.

"I know it sounds like a bother, but Kim will be in charge," Lisa looked over at the manager, a soccer-playing university student that everyone liked, "and you just find her and let her know before you leave, and speak to her when you return."

"So, you'll know who to search if anything else disappears from the dressing room?" said Janice.

A few of the girls gasped.

"No, of course, not," said Lisa, her face flushing. "Believe me, we'd rather not do this, but we have to show that we care and that we are doing something."

A couple of girls glared at Tiana, as though it was her fault that someone took her phone, but no one else made any comment.

"Let's move on now," said Lisa looking relieved and turning to the chalkboard. She began outlining what they were going to try and accomplish at the practice, listing the drills in order, and Rebecca tried hard to listen, but her thoughts were racing.

Was Janice afraid of being searched if something else disappeared? Is that why she asked the question? Can someone be searched without a warrant? She didn't know about that. She began to wish she had mentioned to her mom or dad that she had seen Janice shoplifting on Thursday. Why hadn't she? What kind of stupid loyalty did she have for a teammate she barely knew? Well, of course, she knew Janice better now, and wished she didn't.

When the talk was over, everyone picked up whatever they were taking with them, and moved to the door. Rebecca walked out to the field along with Gen and Matea but she looked back to watch Megan lock the door, and she noticed that Matea was watching, too.

"I wonder who left the field on Wednesday during the practice," said Gen, as the three walked on.

"Megan left to get something from the office, Kim went back to get another couple of soccer balls for one of the drills, and Tori, Janice, and Tiana all went to the restroom," answered Matea promptly.

Gen and Rebecca stared at her in astonishment. "How could you remember all that?" asked Rebecca, noting that Janice was one of the girls who was absent for awhile.

"Tiana and I talked about it all weekend, of course," Matea answered. "It was a major topic of conversation at our house. There may have been other girls who left the field, as well, but those are the only ones we noticed."

"We need a detective," Gen said, as they reached the field, and lined up their water bottles and backpacks. Matea and Rebecca laughed but they weren't laughing the following week when another phone disappeared from the dressing room.

This time, the theft was much more serious. Rebecca was one of the girls who had left the field to use the restroom, and she was suddenly very frightened by what had happened. She would come under suspicion. How horrible was this turn of events?

There was only one answer to this problem and, right after dinner that night, she called Chris and told him she needed the help of the Viking Club Detective Agency.

Chris laughed and then he stopped and there was a moment of silence.

"You mean the detective agency we formed after we figured out who took the Viking Tournament trophy?" he asked cautiously. (See *Something's Missing*, Volume One of the Viking Club Mysteries)

"That's the one," said Rebecca.

Again there was silence. "How about Jaylon? Are you going to call him, too?" he asked finally.

"Yes, I am," Rebecca answered. "He's just a little kid, but you know, he really notices things. Without him, we never would have figured out what happened."

"You're right; he did help a lot."

"It's all hands on deck. I need everybody," said Rebecca.

"Okay, you're on," said Chris. "Name the time and the place."

After a few more minutes of discussion, they had settled on where and when, and a few minutes later, Rebecca was talking to Jaylon.

When he came on the phone, he sounded so young — he was only ten, after all — she almost changed her mind, but then, clinging to the thought that 'he notices things,' she explained that she was calling on the Viking Club Detective Agency to solve another mystery and needed his help.

He answered right away that he would come, and she could hear the grin in his voice.

It was all set. The three of them would meet at the swing set at the elementary school tomorrow at four o'clock in the afternoon, and would talk there.

When Rebecca hung up the phone, she felt better. She had made her first move to solve her problem. She knew Chris and Jaylon would do their best to help her, and she was comforted by the thought.

CHAPTER NINE

A BLISTERING MEMORY

As Jaylon and his dad drove to the soccer practice Sunday evening, Jaylon felt a glow of supreme satisfaction thinking about the phone call that had come just before he left the house. The Viking Club Detective Agency was on a case, and he was going to be part of it. Yes!

He was never sure that the other two really meant to include him in other mystery cases if any came up. Maybe they were just being nice to him after the first mystery was solved, and since they were all together, it would have been difficult to exclude him. But, of course, he had helped solve it — he knew he did — it's just that the other two kids were so much older than he was.

Well, Chris was actually only two years older than Jaylon, now that he thought about it, but Chris was bigger and he *seemed* much older. Jaylon felt proud when Chris spoke to him in the hallway at school after that. He saw Rebecca at a distance now and then, but she was always surrounded by a pack of girls and never noticed him. In September, Chris would be starting his last year at their school before going off to high school for grade eight, but Rebecca was starting high school this very year; she really must think of him as a little kid!

And then he remembered. She had been the one to call him and ask for his help; she was the one with the mystery to solve. So, little kid or not, she thought he was okay, and Jaylon smiled to himself, and wondered what the mystery was. He hoped he would be able to help. Maybe he would even solve it for them! He wished he could tell his dad but Rebecca said that they should keep their investigations private.

"We'll call on help from the adults when we have a case but, for now, we want to keep everything to ourselves. Detectives work better when they're undercover, don't you agree?" she had asked him and, of course, he agreed. What she said made a lot of sense.

As the soccer practice got underway, Jaylon realized he had his own mystery to solve. Again he was outrunning

Patrick and beating him to the ball every time. Was it a joke? Why was Patrick letting him win?

After the fourth race for the ball had ended by Jaylon reaching it first and getting his kick away, Pat was still a couple of paces behind him. Was Patrick smiling? Jaylon gave Patrick a sharp look, and, no, he wasn't smiling. In fact, he wouldn't meet Jaylon's eye and walked away before Jaylon could ask him what had happened. And was he limping again? Yes, he wa...no, he wasn't.

Finally, Jaylon realized what he was seeing. Patrick limped *some* of the time, but not *most* of the time. Why would that be? Jaylon remembered two summer ago when he put on his runners from the year before. His mom looked at him after he took a few steps and then reached down and squeezed the toes of the runners.

"Too small," she announced. "You're outgrowing everything, even your shoes. I'll take you shopping on the weekend and we'll get you a new pair of runners."

"I'm going to wear these to Edward's house, though," Jaylon said, looking down at them. He liked his summer runners even if they were too small.

"No, don't," Mom advised. "You'll get blisters if you do and blisters really hurt."

Jaylon had never had a blister and didn't care if he did have one. How bad could a blister be? He wore the shoes to Edward's house without his mom noticing, and found out. Blisters hurt a lot! He limped home from Edward's after a couple of hours, and wished he had listened to his mom.

In fact, he felt like an idiot and his mom would wonder why he done something so stupid after what she'd told him. When he arrived home, he steeled himself to walk normally and hoped he could escape to his bedroom without his mom or his dad — who was probably home by now — noticing that he walked with a limp. It was tough but he did it and, with great relief, took his shoes off when he reached the safety of his room. Made it!

Not quite. He wore only his socks around the house for the rest of the evening but, in the morning, he had to put on his regular shoes again, and they hurt almost as much as the runners! He had to admit to his mom what he had done and showed her the blisters on his feet.

"Oh, Jaylon, do you have to learn everything the hard way?" Mom asked. "These blisters will take awhile to heal. You'll have to wear band aids over all these red spots, as well as over the blisters, and take them off at night and then put new band aids on in the morning before you put on your shoes until your feet heal."

"Okay, Mom, I'm sorry," Jaylon said mournfully.

"If I tell you not to walk off a cliff because you'll get hurt if you do, are you going walk off anyway?"

"No-o-o-o-o, Mom!" Jaylon said, half laughing.

"All right," said Mom, "I'm just checking. I want to know if we need to buy a truckload of band aids for the summer."

However, she said nothing more about it after that one time. She knew he had learned his lesson.

Someone's Trapped

However, what was going on with Patrick? No soccer player would ever wear cleats that didn't fit and get blisters if he could avoid it, which meant that, for some reason, Patrick couldn't avoid it.

As soon as the practice was over and he was back in the car, Jaylon told his dad all about it.

"That's really sad," said Dad, shaking his head, " but I can't say that I'm surprised. Patrick's dad was laid off at the plant when they closed part of it down, and I guess when you saw him at the park, he was probably trying to get a job there. There aren't many jobs around right now, and money must be very tight at their house."

"So, they don't have enough money to buy him new cleats?"

"Very likely that's it."

"But he's on the team and you said it was expensive to play soccer on the international team."

"It is," Dad said, "but there was a scholarship fund for each age group, and one person on each team gets to play without paying the fees. The winners were announced in the newspaper, don't you remember? Patrick won because he was the top scorer in your age group city-wide, and you know one of the other winners, too — Chris Canic."

"Yes," said Jaylon, "I know him, and I remember now about the scholarships."

"Maybe Mr. MacLaren will have a job soon," Dad said, "and Patrick will be able to get some new cleats."

"But what if he can't? Can't we buy him some cleats?"

"I would buy them if his family would let me give him a pair," Dad said seriously, "but they won't. People won't let you do things like that for them. It's one thing to have to accept food, medical aid, or items that you can't do without. People will swallow their pride and take something like that, but soccer cleats? Patrick's parents would be very upset if I even offered. It would be insulting to them."

"But we have to do something," said Jaylon, torn by the memory of what blisters felt like, and Patrick's efforts not to show he was in pain. Patrick's feet must be covered in band aids.

"If you can think of some way of getting him some cleats that doesn't involve charity — a handout — come and tell me what it is, and I'll do it," said Dad. "I will; I promise."

Jaylon had to be satisfied with that. He spent the rest of the drive home trying to come up with a plan, but couldn't figure out a thing. Some detective he was!

CHAPTER TEN

TOO MANY SUSPECTS

Rebecca was the first one at the meeting spot the next day, and took a seat on a swing. There were little children playing on the small jungle gym not far away with their moms seated on a park bench watching them, but she was the only one at the swings right now. They could always move the meeting to some other spot if necessary; it was a big schoolyard. She could see Jaylon coming up one walkway and Chris approaching from the other.

"Good, everyone from the agency is here," Rebecca said after they had all greeted each other, Jaylon a bit shyly. "I'm glad you came. I'll tell you what the problem is and then you both go ahead and ask me anything. I don't expect a solution today, or even a plan, but if we talk about it for awhile maybe we can think of something to work on and we can meet later in the week and see if we can't figure out what to do."

"Sounds okay to me," said Chris taking a seat on one of the swings next to her.

Jaylon sat down on a patch of grass facing them.

Rebecca decided to tell the story just as it had unfolded for her, beginning with the story of the first missing phone and then went on to tell them how she discovered her teammate was a thief who had stolen a t-shirt from a store. She wound it up with the theft of the second phone and why she knew she was a suspect. Even if no other phones were stolen, if no one ever found out who took them, there are people who would never trust her again.

There was silence after she finished, and Rebecca sat and waited for the questions. Chris was first.

"How many people had an opportunity to take both phones. Who from your team was gone both times?" Chris asked.

"Megan, the assistant coach; Kim, the manager; and the players, Janice, Tiana, and Tori."

"So, why would you be a suspect?" asked Jaylon. "You couldn't have taken the first phone."

"Yes, but I'm the only one who knows that. Matea said those were the only names she and Tiana could come up with that first time, but they know someone else could have left the field without their noticing. No one was keeping track then."

"We should be able to eliminate Tiana," said Jaylon. "Her phone was the first one stolen."

"No one searched Tiana's things, I'll bet," said Chris immediately. "What if it's a cover? She pretends her phone was stolen so no one will suspect her if she takes the second one."

"I suppose that's possible but it's pretty twisted," said Rebecca. "Tiana is without a phone right now. What would be the point?"

"You think it was Janice, don't you?" said Jaylon.

"Yes," said Rebecca simply.

"Why didn't you tell anyone when you discovered she had taken the t-shirt? I can see why you wouldn't say anything at the store, but why didn't you tell your mom or dad when you got home? It wasn't your fault," said Jaylon.

"I should have done something at the time and I didn't know what to do. And my mom would have phoned Janice's mom because if I ever did anything like that she would want to know so she could do something about it — make me take counseling or something.

"If my mom phoned, Janice would know that I had ratted her out and she would hate me. Who knows what would happen after that? She has a lot of friends who will be at high school next year. I'll run into them in

September...." Rebecca's voice trailed off as she suddenly realized she might start to cry if she kept talking.

The boys were quiet for a minute while she pulled herself together.

Chris started again. "Janice will know something's up if you keep avoiding her. She might suspect you saw her take the t-shirt, in which case, she's probably afraid you'll stand up in the dressing room and accuse her of stealing the phones, too."

"Is she poor?" asked Jaylon, suddenly thinking of Patrick who couldn't afford new cleats.

Rebecca shook her head. "No, the family is loaded. You should see the great pool they have in the backyard. The whole house is a showpiece."

"What if her dad lost his job?" said Jaylon still thinking of Patrick. "They might have the house but no money."

"Do you know someone in that situation?" Chris asked, suddenly wondering if Jaylon's dad had lost his job. Chris couldn't remember where Mr. Wilson worked.

"Yeah, I do. It's horrible. The best player on our team can't afford new cleats and he's running half as fast as he used to run because his feet hurt so much. He doesn't want anyone to know, but I found out. I asked my dad if he could buy them for him and he said he can't because Patrick's dad was laid off from his job and it would insult Patrick's family if he offered. Dad said if I want him to have new cleats, I have to come up with a plan. Patrick is my good friend. I don't know what to do."

"That's tough," said Chris, shaking his head. "You're sure that's not the case with Janice?" he asked, looking at Rebecca.

"No, they have lots of money. I know they have," said Rebecca. "She's probably stealing for kicks."

"Why don't you tell your mom and dad now that the second phone has disappeared and you are a suspect? That's pretty scary," said Jaylon.

"Same answer as before," said Rebecca a bit impatiently. "Nothing has changed in the last five minutes."

"What has happened with Janice in the meantime?" asked Chris. "Is she still trying to be friends with you?"

"No, she's invited me three times to go to her house for a swim or to go someplace with her and I have always given her an excuse as to why I can't go. After the third time, she stopped asking me, but we still say 'Hi' when we see each other. I don't believe she knows I saw her take the t-shirt."

"Suppose it wasn't Janice who took the phone. We know it wasn't you, and it probably wasn't Tiana, either. Tell us about the others who had the opportunity," said Chris.

"You mean tell you about the assistant coach, the manager, and Tori?"

"Yeah, those," said Chris.

"The only one I really know well is Tori, who's captain of our hockey team, and I've known her for a long time. We don't hang out because we go to different schools, but she's nice and she's friendly." Rebecca shrugged. "Also, we've never lost anything from our hockey team dressing rooms."

"Wait a minute, what if it isn't someone who's on your team?" said Jaylon. "There could be another key and it could be someone from another team or anyone who goes into the clubhouse now and then who took the phones."

"True," said Chris, "however, if that's the case, why aren't phones disappearing from that dressing room when other teams are using it? I haven't heard anything about phones being stolen."

"Yeah," said Jaylon, "I guess we have to set something up so we can keep watch on that dressing room whenever Rebecca's team is playing or practicing."

"What?" Rebecca and Chris spoke at the exact same time.

"Chris and I will have to watch the door and see who goes into your dressing room when your team is practicing or playing a game," said Jaylon with a shrug. "How else are we going to find out?"

"We'd have to do that without being seen," said Chris thoughtfully. "How could we do that?"

"I don't know," said Jaylon. "Isn't there stuff around, like cameras, and recording machines that we can use? There are computers that have that spy stuff on them, too. I've seen them on TV programs."

"I think the CIA would have no problems solving this mystery, but unless you can get your hands on something like that and know how to set it up, I'd say we're done," said Chris with a grin. "I don't have any CIA connections."

"Well, then, we'll have to figure out how to watch the room ourselves," said Jaylon reasonably. "What else is there to do?"

There was a moment of silence while they thought that over.

"You're right," announced Chris. "That's what we have to do. I have a practice on Tuesday night. How about you, Jaylon?"

"Wednesday at five o'clock."

"Let's check everything out and see if we can come up with any ideas on what we can do." He turned to Rebecca. "Which dressing room does your team use?"

"It's number 113," said Rebecca, suddenly hopeful. "Do you think we can figure something out?"

"That's the one around the corner off that long hallway at the back, right?"

"Yes."

"Well, I guess it will be up to Jaylon and me to watch the room, but you look over everything from the inside and around the dressing room and help us figure out how we can do that. When's your next practice?"

"We have a game on Wednesday."

"Okay, you do your checking then. We need a sketch of the inside of the dressing room, and the girl's restroom, windows, all that stuff."

"Why? Are you going to hide somewhere?"

"Well, not in the girl's restroom, I hope, but somewhere. I don't know how we can do this yet," said Chris. "We need more data."

"Yeah, the data. That's what we're missing," Jaylon said. "Where's the data on that? Gimme a little data."

And suddenly, they were all laughing.

"Hand over the data and no one will get hurt."

"Step away from the data, and put your hands in the air."

"A little data here, a little data there; here a data, there a data...."

Rebecca started to giggle. She felt a whole lot better. Finally, they all managed to stop laughing.

"I've seen you at the clubhouse. How's your team doing?" said Rebecca, smiling at Jaylon.

"We're doing well," said Jaylon enthusiastically. "We've won our first few games. So, if we can keep it up, we'll get into the playoffs this year."

"Awesome," said Rebecca.

"Good for you," said Chris.

"And you, too," Rebecca said, looking at Chris. "I've seen you a couple of times at the clubhouse. How is your team doing?"

"Okay. We're doing okay. We haven't had any phones stolen yet."

Rebecca made a face at him. "Well, congratulations on making that team. The guys are all older than you, aren't they? That was pretty brilliant of you."

"Yeah," said Chris looking off into space.

"Why won't your teammates pass you the ball?" asked Jaylon as he picked up a stick and began idly tossing it from one hand to another.

"What?" said Rebecca, staring a Jaylon. "What did you say?"

"My dad and I saw a game. I had just finished playing — and we won our game — and so we stayed to watch Chris's game. No one on his team would pass Chris the ball even when he was open. My dad says something's going on." Jaylon looked at Chris. "What's up?"

Chris shrugged. "I guess the guys weren't happy to hear that I was such a prize they should all be like me. They should all work harder or I'd show them up."

"So, who's your idiot coach?" said Rebecca, very angry.

"Oh, he's a nice guy."

"No, he's not; he's an idiot. What's his name?"

"Are you going to find him and beat him up?"

Rebecca grinned, "You never know your luck."

"Jerry Cartwright."

"He's allowing all that to happen to you. It's called bullying. He's letting it happen."

"I don't think he's noticed."

"Of course he's noticed."

Chris shrugged. "Nothing I can do. Anyway we have a mystery to solve," he stood up, "and I have to get home."

"So do I," said Jaylon, getting to his feet. "When do we meet again?"

"Is Thursday okay with everyone? It will give us all a chance to look things over."

Everyone agreed that Thursday was fine — same time, same place.

They started to leave and Chris suddenly paused and said, "Jaylon, your friend who needs the soccer shoes?"

"Yeah?"

"Have a draw; everybody puts their name in a box. The story is that a sporting goods store wants a little publicity so they are going to hold a draw for a couple of teams. Yours has been chosen first. The prize will be a pair of cleats and the lucky winner gets to go to the store and pick them out within a certain price range. Your dad can probably arrange that with the coach and some store, right?"

"Yes," said Jaylon, wide eyed. "But how can we be sure Patrick's name will be drawn?"

Chris and Rebecca both laughed. "It's a matter of having two identical boxes for the draw," Chris explained. "Everyone puts their name in one box and when it's time for the draw, you pull out an identical looking box."

"It's the old switch-the-box trick," said Rebecca. "In the second box, all the entries have the same name: Patrick. No matter which entry is pulled, he wins."

"That's right. It's the old switcheroo," said Chris.

"The switcheroo," echoed Rebecca.

"Alright! Thank you," said Jaylon, very happy. "I'll tell my dad."

Someone's Trapped

"Don't forget the name — it's the switcheroo!"

The three parted but kept looking back and calling out "switcheroo" until they lost sight of each other.

It was altogether a good meeting.

CHAPTER ELEVEN

PLANS UNFOLD

When the three members of the Viking Detective Agency met again, Rebecca was already seated at the same swing when the boys arrived. There was no one else nearby. Rebecca had two rough floor plan drawings, which she handed to Chris — one of the interior of the dressing room, and the second of the hallway, with doors indicated, the rooms identified, and showing one window at the end of the long hall.

Chris took the drawings and sat down on the grass beside Jaylon and the two boys carefully examined them. After a moment, Chris took the plans, folded them in half, folded them again, and stuffed them into his pocket.

He stood up and moved to the swing beside Rebecca, where he had been sitting at Monday's meeting, and took his seat. Jaylon remained on the grass.

Chris idly swung back and forth, deep in thought, until Rebecca couldn't stand it any longer.

"Well?" she demanded, "have you nothing to say?" She looked over at Jaylon. "Either of you?"

"You don't have a drawing of the interior of the girls' restroom," Chris said finally. "Didn't we mention we needed that?"

"What? Seriously? Are you kidding me? You can't mean that," Rebecca said, genuinely horrified.

Chris exploded into laughter and Jaylon joined in.

"We were looking forward to seeing a drawing of the girls' restroom, that's all," Chris said, when he could finally talk. "We're a bit disappointed."

"Yeah, that could have been the important data we needed," said Jaylon with a big grin.

"If you want to see what the girls' restroom looks like, I'll give you both a guided tour," said Rebecca, refusing to smile. Didn't these two zombies know how serious the situation was? Were stupid jokes all they had for her?

"We don't need the tour, thanks, all the same," Chris said, "but your drawings are incomplete. You forgot to include the most important item. Fortunately, Jaylon and I found exactly what we need. I'll keep the floor plans in case one of us writes a book about all the mysteries we've solved together. They might be useful."

"We're going to solve this one?" said Rebecca with a surge of hope.

"Sure we are," said Chris. "When's your next practice? We can't do this at a game."

"It's Sunday night at seven o'clock."

"Are you available Sunday at seven o'clock?" Chris said to Jaylon. "And can your dad pick us up after Rebecca's practice is over?"

"Yes, I'm sure my dad will pick us up. Do you want me to get my dad to drive us there, too?"

"I don't think so. We're better off not having to explain anything until we're finished. If we're successful, we'll need somebody's dad, and I'm all out of dads right now. Or a mom will do. My mom is pretty tied up, too, and I'd just as soon it stayed that way as long as possible."

Rebecca nodded sympathetically. "My dad and my mom will help," she said. "What it is? What are you going to do?"

"Does one of your parents usually drive you to practice?"

"Yes, my mom does. What is it? What do you need?"

Chris hesitated. "We'll tell you the plan," he said finally, "and you tell us what you think of how we want to wrap it up. Jaylon's dad should probably be the one to help us since he helped us the last time we solved a mystery. Jaylon and I will come to your practice by bus, and then have Jaylon's dad pick us up. We'll ask him to come a bit early. If we have our evidence, he's the

Someone's Trapped **89**

outsider, not connected to your team, who could be there while we explain, but having someone from your family there is okay, too. I just don't want anyone knowing about this until we have the evidence. They'll probably try to stop us."

"Yes, yes, sure," said Rebecca impatiently. "Whatever you like. Just tell me."

"Okay," said Chris, "here's what we're going to do."

And he laid out the plan for her.

"You're crazy," she exclaimed, when he finished. "Seriously. How can you think of doing such a thing?"

"It's not crazy. It's going to work."

Rebecca looked at Jaylon. "You're really going to be able to do that?"

"Sure," he said with a grin. "Piece of cake."

Chris said, "He's the only one of us who can. Let's hope our thief makes a move on Sunday night and it will be all over. If not, we have to go through this again."

"Oh, no," moaned Rebecca, "I can't let you do this."

"We're doing it. You just remember what you have to do, and let us worry about the rest. Anyway, nothing is carved in stone. We can always change the plan if anything goes wrong."

"Hey, my dad liked your plan about the draw for the cleats," Jaylon said suddenly. "He's going to do it. Our team has a practice next Monday night, and he's hoping to have all the arrangements made by then. We can have the draw after the practice."

"That's epic," said Chris with a broad smile. "Your dad is a good guy."

"He is; he is," said Rebecca. "Maybe it's a sign. Maybe everything is going to work for us on all fronts. Maybe we can't lose."

"I think it's a sign, too," said Jaylon solemnly. "The Viking Detective Agency scores and we'll score again Sunday night."

He stood and put his hand out towards them, palm down, and the other two each stood up, placed a hand on top of his.

"Go Vikings!" he called out.

"Go Vikings!" they yelled in unison.

"See you Sunday night," said Chris, pulling his hand away.

"Sunday night," the other two responded, and they went their separate ways.

CHAPTER TWELVE

LOCKED AND LOADED

Sunday night, the two boys, dressed in their soccer jerseys and Chris with a backpack slung over his shoulder, made their way to the clubhouse from the bus stop. Jaylon didn't usually ride a bus and he thought it was a cool way to get around.

"It's not that great in the winter, or when it's raining," Chris pointed out after Jaylon's third exclamation of how great it was to ride a bus. "It isn't great when you have a lot to carry either."

"You mean like a hockey bag?" Jalon asked.

"Exactly like a hockey bag."

"I guess that would suck. How much longer is your dad going to be in Afghanistan?"

Chris said, "He comes home on leave in another couple of months, but then he has to go back for another six months."

Jaylon thought that sounded pretty terrible, but said only, "Be nice when it's over."

"Yes," agreed Chris.

They reached the clubhouse and walked through to the exit on the other side, which opened onto a walkway leading out into the field. The stands were to their right and held a sprinkling of parents. To reach the stands, they would have to go back through the clubhouse and to a path that led to the stands.

Chris walked over to an area that separated the stands from the playing field by a mesh fence, leaned up against one of the posts, arms crossed in front of him, and watched the field. With their soccer jerseys on, the boys didn't look out of place.

Jaylon paced back and forth restlessly beside him. "Has she seen us yet?"

"Probably," said Chris. "Don't worry. I see only two adults and I'm guessing there's still someone else in the dressing room along with the assistant manager."

"Unless she didn't come tonight."

"We have a signal for that, remember?"

"Oh, yeah, that's right."

Someone's Trapped   **93**

Maureen Grenier

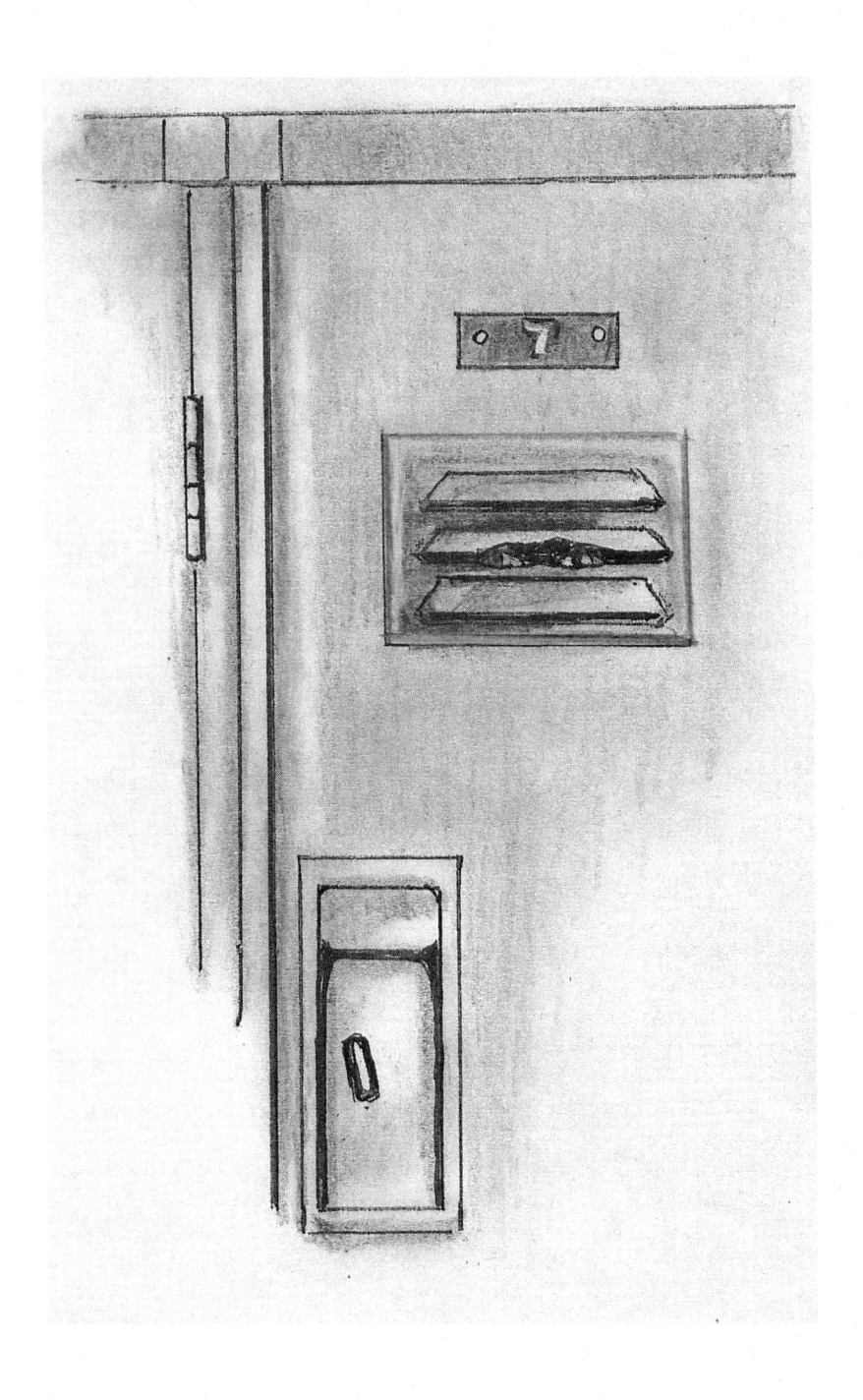

Chris looked over at Jaylon sympathetically. "Are you getting anxious?"

"I'm just anxious to get started," Jaylon answered.

"Soon," said Chris, "soon," and half closed his eyes, relaxing against the fence.

They didn't have long to wait. It was only a couple of minutes later that a woman accompanied by a girl dressed in a practice jersey walked through the doors and out to the field.

"Here we go," said Chris, his eyes fixed on Rebecca. "Wait for it."

Rebecca looked at the two who just joined them on the field, and without looking in the direction of the clubhouse, reached up and pulled her ponytail band off, stretched her hair back again, bunched it together, and replaced the band.

"That's the signal. Everybody is here," Chris straightened up, turned, and drifted back through the doors with Jaylon behind him.

"When we start down the corridor, head straight to the window at the end, in case anyone is in the hall and sees us."

"What are we going to do at the window?"

"Look outside, I guess. What else do you do at a window?"

Jaylon started to giggle. "No one will wonder why we walked down the hall to look out the window instead of going the other way and looking out the door instead?"

Someone's Trapped **95**

"Actually, there's something on the windowsill that we have to pick up."

"Yeah?" said Jaylon. "What if it's not there?"

"It'll be there," Chris said opening his hand and showing him a referee's whistle on a black ribbon. "My friend asked me to get this for her. She left it behind after the last game. She remembers leaving it on the windowsill."

"Why was your friend, the ref, looking out the window?"

"Beats me. Who knows why girls do anything?" said Chris.

They were heading down the hall now and, since no one was around, they didn't need the whistle excuse. Chris put it in his pocket, just in case someone came along, and then opened his backpack. After another quick look around, he stopped half way down the corridor and opened one of the lockers in the bank of old lockers facing the two dressing rooms in the corridor. None of them were locked. The lockers had not been noted by Rebecca in her drawings, probably because she couldn't possibly fit into one, just as Chris couldn't either. Fortunately, Jaylon could.

Jaylon pulled his phone out of his pocket, turned and backed into the locker, and was able to stand upright. "Good thing you took the shelf out," he said. "This is going to be fine. Better be quick."

Chris handed him a water bottle that Jaylon shoved into the pocket of his shorts and then he placed an empty, wide-mouthed can between Jaylon's feet.

"What's the can for?" Jaylon asked in surprise.

"That's in case someone scares the piss out of you," Chris said. "Once I close the door, you won't be able to get out. The can is for emergency purposes."

Jaylon was laughing as Chris shut the door.

"Are you sure you're okay?" Chris asked, worried now that the moment had come and he was going to leave Jaylon trapped in the locker.

"Yeah, I'm fine."

Chris could see the glitter of Jaylon's eyes between two of the air slits, which Chris had widened Tuesday night with the screwdriver attached to his Swiss army knife. "Make sure you can get the phone up and the angle will be okay to take the video."

Obediently, Jaylon moved his phone into position. "Oh, no, there's something in the way." His voice sounded muffled.

"What it is it?" asked Chris, alarmed.

"It's you," said Jaylon, pulling the phone down. "Go away before someone finds you talking to a locker and thinks you're a nut case."

"Okay," Chris laughed, feeling better. "I'll be watching and I'll come and check on you when I can."

"Awesome," was Jaylon's response.

Chris walked away, wishing he could have been the one in the locker. However, Jaylon seemed perfectly fine with the possibility of spending an hour and a half in that cramped space and insisted that he was an experienced cameraman, and his phone was fully charged. If anyone entered the dressing room, Jaylon would capture it on film. They all had their fingers crossed that the thief would strike again tonight.

"If only," Chris thought to himself as he walked out of the building and up into the stands. He sat near the bottom, and watched the action on the field, wondering which one was Janice, the t-shirt thief. There were four girls on the team with long, blond hair. He checked his watch and realized this was going to be a long practice no matter how much time it took or didn't take. Being a detective wasn't nearly as much fun as he once thought. It was mostly just nerve wracking. Forty minutes into the practice, he realized it was also pretty boring.

CHAPTER THIRTEEN

TRAPPED

Chris checked his watch again and decided he had better go and see how Jaylon was doing even though no one had left the field yet. Maybe the thief wasn't going to strike tonight, or maybe they were all wrong and the thief wasn't a member of Rebecca's team after all. What if there wasn't enough light coming from that window and a video captured by Jaylon's phone wasn't going to be clear enough? He squinted up at the sun. Nah, it was still very bright; however, he'd better check on his 'prisoner' in the locker just the same.

He stood up and, as soon as he did, saw a girl with long blond hair leaving the field. Chris leaned over and pretended to pick up something from the stairs beside him and then sat back down. Could this be Janice? Chris kept his face turned to the field but his eyes followed the progress of the blond until she disappeared from sight into the clubhouse.

He sat and waited for what seemed like a very long time until she reappeared, jogging her way back onto the field. He let out a long breath and realized he had been holding if for awhile. If she took a phone while she was in there, she would have had to stash it somewhere until she could safely smuggle it out of the clubhouse. She certainly didn't have anything in either hand when she came back to the field, but it could be wrapped in something in a locker in the dressing room. She could probably stick in her backpack and walk out of there without any problem. No one was searching any personal belongings and probably wouldn't unless the police became involved.

Chris couldn't stand it any longer. He took one more look at the field and started down the stairs. He paused at the bottom and then moved towards the fence and stood there. Someone else had left the field — a woman. He moved farther along the first row and took a seat. As she drew close to the clubhouse, he could see her clearly. He knew this was the assistant coach, Megan, the one who locked up and had the key to the dressing room. Maybe this was their thief.

He settled down for another wait and suddenly his attention was caught by what was happening on the field.

They were starting a trapping drill and he knew the play well. He often tried to intercept a pass with his chest so that he could hunch his shoulders forward to trap the ball and direct the it down to his feet so that he could play it. It was a very useful skill for someone who couldn't get a pass from his teammates. And how great was this? The team was practicing 'trapping' the ball on the field while the Viking Detective Agency was 'trapping' a thief in the dressing room. It was Chris's favorite kind of joke.

Megan, on their list of suspects, reappeared and rejoined the team on the field. Chris decided to wait a few more minutes, just to be safe, and ten minutes later, he saw Rebecca start towards the clubhouse. He was stunned. Rebecca had told them she wouldn't leave the field unless it was at gunpoint and, as she drew closer he could see that she was very upset. He stood up, and she saw him. He didn't wait for any kind of signal but turned and headed towards the clubhouse as fast as he could move and when he got inside he could see her coming down the hall. He raced towards her.

"What happened? Why are you in here?"

"Megan sent me to get something from the dressing room." She held up the key and looked like she was going to cry.

"Don't worry, we'll get it all taped," Chris said reassuringly as he ran down the hall ahead of her.

"Jaylon, Jaylon, we need you out here," he called. He reached the locker and opened it to a very surprised looking Jaylon.

"Come out, you need to record this," Chris ordered. "Rebecca is being set up."

Jaylon obediently stepped out, lifted his phone, and started videotaping.

Rebecca reached the door to the dressing room.

Chris stepped forward and into the picture and said, " So, tell us, Rebecca, why are you going into the dressing room?" He motioned to her to unlock the door.

"Megan told me to get some pills from her jacket. She has a headache. She gave me the key," Rebecca answered looking anxiously towards the phone camera.

"You know we are filming here because we are hoping to trap the person who is stealing the phones, don't you?" Chris continued.

"Yes, I know," Rebecca answered, "but what else could I do?"

"Nothing. Get the pills and Jaylon will film you while you are in there."

"And move it," added Jaylon, "I'm running out of juice here."

"Okay," Rebecca answered, and hurried inside. She found the jacket and removed a little container of pills from one of the pockets.

"Quickly, quickly," urged Jaylon.

"I'm coming," said Rebecca as she ran back to them, pulled the door closed and relocked it.

"Now, run," said Chris. "We want to show you leaving the building. Go, go, go!"

Rebecca turned and raced down the hall and around the corner with the two boys running behind her, Jaylon filming. She fled down the second hall and out into the sunlight.

"Cut," said Chris, and he and Jaylon immediately doubled up laughing.

"So, I can't wait," said Chris when he could talk. "Did you get Megan, our master criminal, going into the dressing room earlier?"

"I did."

"Did anyone else go in?"

"No."

"I think we got her, Watson."

"Why am I Watson? Why aren't I Sherlock?"

Again, they burst out laughing.

"Okay, you can be Sherlock for this one," said Chris wiping his eyes. "You deserve it. Have you got any room left on your phone?"

"A little," Jaylon said, after a quick check.

"Okay. You'd better go back in the locker until the end of the game, just in case anyone else shows up. We have to be ready for all contingencies," said Chris as they started back down the long hall.

"Contingencies? If I'm going to record contingencies, you'd better tell me what contingencies are. I may have already missed a bunch of contingencies."

Chris laughed. "'Contingencies' means 'possibilities.'" He looked at his watch. "I think you're probably going to have a very boring ten minutes. I hope you have a little room left on the phone to tape when the girls come back to the dressing room. Just record a bit of that and then close it down. I'll come for you right after, and your dad will be around, too."

Jaylon backed into the locker again and Chris shut the door.

"See you later. Won't be long now," said Chris as he turned to go back up the hall.

"Okay, I'll just wait here and videotape contingencies until you get back," came the muffled reply.

CHAPTER FOURTEEN

SHOWDOWN

When Chris got back to the stands, Jaylon's dad was seated a few rows up and smiled when he saw Chris.

"Hi, Mr. Wilson," said Chris, mounting the steps and taking a seat beside him.

"So, Jaylon told me you have some big caper on tonight," said Mr. Wilson. "Are you three kids catching bad guys again?"

"No, we're not catching bad guys," said Chris.

Mr. Wilson nodded, smiled, and resumed watching the practice.

"Bad girls."

"Oh," said Mr. Wilson, and then paused, turned his head and looked more closely at Chris. "What was that?"

"Bad girls. We're catching bad *girls* this time."

Mr. Wilson said, "Okay, I'm listening."

So, Chris explained what the problem was and how they had chosen to solve it, but he kept an eye on the field to see if anyone else approached the clubhouse before the end of the practice. Mr. Wilson listened carefully, his eyes never leaving Chris's face.

"So, you're telling me that Jaylon is still in a locker?" he asked when Chris had finished.

"Yes, we thought it was best to wait until the practice was over and the girls returned and he could get a shot of the first girls going into the dressing room."

"What if no phone is stolen?"

"Then we have to do this again at the next practice."

Mr. Wilson buried his head in his hands for a moment, and then looked up at Chris again. "Isn't there an easier way?"

"Like what?" asked Chris. "We couldn't think of anything."

"Well, there is equipment that can do that; equipment that can keep an eye on a door or a room."

"Can you do that in a public place without running into a legal problem?"

"No, but you aren't exactly providing real evidence and I'm not sure what you are doing is legal either."

"Well, we're kids — what do we know?" grinned Chris. "That's why we didn't tell you or any other adult ahead of time. If it doesn't work this time, we have to do it again, and you have to forget you ever heard this conversation."

Chris added, "And we don't need to have anything to take into court. We just have to make sure everyone knows our friend Rebecca isn't a thief. If a phone has been stolen tonight — and the very fact that Rebecca was sent to the dressing room with a key makes us pretty sure she is being set up — you can bet Megan will insist that it isn't legal to conduct a search. If she's the thief, she'll want Rebecca to leave without being searched so that she can never prove her innocence. We need to have the girls and the coach see the tape. What the adults chose to do about the theft is up to them."

Chris rose to his feet and gestured to the field. "They're getting ready to come off. I have to go and let Jaylon out in a minute. We'll wait at the end of the hall. If a phone has been stolen, Rebecca will come to the door to get us right away."

Mr. Wilson stood up, too. "Shouldn't I be there?"

"Come down but stay in the main hall. If nothing has happened, it's best if you aren't involved in case we have to do this again."

"This puts me in a very awkward position, Chris," Mr. Wilson began.

"Don't worry. We think this will all be over soon. If we need you, just be there. You don't have to say anything.

Someone's Trapped **107**

We need to show this tape to the girls and the coach. It would be nice if you were there, in case the coach won't listen."

Without waiting for a response, Chris turned and ran down the steps and hurried into the clubhouse. The girls came streaming by a few minutes later and he saw Mr. Wilson come into the clubhouse and station himself by the bulletin board, where he began to read the announcements and articles posted on it with what seemed to be a great deal of interest. Chris headed for the long hall and waited at the corner. As soon as the coast was clear, he moved on down and let Jaylon out of the locker. They walked a few steps away.

"Anyone else come by?"

"Nope. Is my dad here?"

"Yes, he's going to wait until we need him. If Rebecca comes out into the hall to get us, you call me, and I'll stick my head around the corner and tell him. He'll come to the dressing room with us but I'll do the talking."

"What if some girls leave without checking to see if a phone or anything else is missing?"

"Rebecca will see that doesn't happen, remember?" Chris said, backing away and up the hall. "She'll announce that her stuff is disturbed and tell them she's looking to see if anything is taken and will suggest they look at their things, too."

"Oh, yeah, I forgot," Jaylon said absently as he checked his phone. "Hey, this film looks pretty good!"

Chris paused. "You mean, 'Hollywood, here I come'?"

"Maybe."

They both laughed and then Chris continued on his way and positioned himself at the corner. The moment of truth was approaching. What was it going to be?

Moments later, Rebecca burst out of the dressing room, spotted Jaylon and called to him, "Another phone has been stolen!"

"We're on our way!" Jaylon called back.

Rebecca went back inside and closed the door; Jaylon stepped around the corner and called to Chris, "We're on!"

Chris stuck his head around the next corner and called, "Mr. Wilson, it's a go!"

They gathered at the door of the dressing room and Chris knocked. Rebecca was waiting just inside and opened it right away.

"Hi," said Chris with a grin, "could we have a word with your coach?"

Rebecca nodded, but Coach Lisa heard the request, and said to Rebecca, "Tell whoever it is, to wait until we are finished here."

Mr. Wilson stepped to the door, pushed it open a little wider, and spoke to the coach. "This can't wait, I'm afraid."

Coach Lisa looked annoyed, but said, "Very well," and moved to the door. Rebecca held it open as the coach stepped out into the hall and then pulled it shut, leaving the coach alone with Mr. Wilson, Chris, and Jaylon.

Someone's Trapped **109**

Mr. Wilson said, "Thank you. These young people here have something to tell you and to show you. Chris and Jaylon, explain to the coach what you've done and why."

And so they did.

CHAPTER FIFTEEN

THE VIKING CLUB AGENCY SCORES AGAIN

Chris sat sucking on a piece of orange and guzzling water while he waited for the second half of the game to begin. Everyone on his team was keyed up. This was the first game of the two-day tournament against the American team and the score was tied. The stands were full of fans, including his mom who had arranged a babysitter for his sisters and was sitting with a neighbor she had brought with her. As well, he saw Jaylon and Mr. Wilson, along with one of Jaylon's friends — probably Patrick.

He grinned up at them and waved when he came off the field at the start of the half-time break. Coming up with a solution to getting Patrick a new pair of cleats was a major success for the Viking Club Detective Agency. Mr. Wilson had used his magic and his money, a person unconnected to the team pulled the winning name out of the box, and presto! Patrick had the cleats he so desperately needed.

Rebecca was up in the stands, too, and Chris waved to her as well. She had brought some of her friends from the soccer team with her and they were not only cheering the team, they were cheering him and calling out his name at every opportunity. There were some older boys from the high school soccer team there also and a few times one of them had screamed out, "Pass it to Chris, you dummy. Can't you see he's open?"

Since Chris had never seen the boy in his life, he assumed this was also something Rebecca had arranged. He was sure that was why his teammates had started passing him the ball, just as if he were a regular team member, which was so rare, it surprised him each time it happened. It certainly paid to have a few fans.

He saw Janice was one of the girls sitting with Rebecca. After the mystery of the phone thefts was cleared up, Rebecca finally had the courage to speak to Janice. She told Janice she had seen her take the t-shirt and had believed she was probably responsible for taking the phones as well.

At first, Janice was indignant and shouted at Rebecca, "How could you think I would steal from my friends?"

Rebecca responded mildly, "Why would you steal from anyone when you have enough money to buy what you want? I don't understand what makes you steal or what rules you have about stealing. How could I know? I didn't tell anyone on the team that you were a thief."

Janice blinked back tears. "I'm not a thief!"

Rebecca put her hand on Janice's arm. "I know you don't want to be a thief. You need to do something about this to make it stop.'

Janice gave a long, shuddering sigh. "I am doing something. I'm seeing someone every week who is trying to help me stop."

Rebecca face broadened into a big smile. "That's great, Janice. You'll be fine. Good for you."

Janice gave her a tearful smile. "Are we still friends?"

"Of course," Rebecca said.

When Rebecca told Jaylon and Chris what happened, Jaylon immediately said, "Are you going to go shopping with her again?"

"Well, no," admitted Rebecca, "but I don't think she'll invite me to go shopping with her anymore."

"Good," said Chris. "Did you ever hear what happened with Megan?"

"Nothing much," Rebecca said. "She disappeared from the team, but I don't know if she was ever charged with anything."

"She wasn't," said Jaylon. "My dad said that even though what we did was enough to get her kicked out of the soccer world, we didn't have the kind of proof you can take into a courtroom. So, the police were told everything, saw the videotape, talked to her about the missing phones afterwards, but they didn't do anything."

Maureen Grenier

"I'll bet the police scared her though. We might have saved her from a life of crime," said Chris. "And I think we should make Mr. Wilson an honorary member of the agency. He gave us the help we needed for the second time."

"Nah, don't bother," said Jaylon. "He was happy to help and thinks we did a good job, but told me to be careful around you two or I might get into some serious trouble someday, and not to take any chances."

The three of them laughed their heads off and Chris said, "Okay, we won't tell him it was your idea to spy on the dressing room door or that it was your idea to hide in the locker."

"Yeah, we won't let him know that we are always very careful around you so that you don't lead us into serious trouble," said Rebecca.

And they laughed some more.

They all agreed that the whole thing was a great triumph for the Viking Club Detective Agency and renewed their promises of calling on each other if another mystery cropped up that needed their attention.

Chris looked up at the stands and remembered that he had thought at the beginning of the soccer season that he should call upon the Viking Club Detectives to help him solve the mystery of how to get his teammates to pass the ball to him. He didn't do that, but his friends were here, doing their best to help him anyway.

The whistle blew signaling the start of the second half and he ran out onto the field with his teammates, and concentrated on playing his best.

When it was down to the last minute or two of play, both teams were feeling discouraged. A tie wasn't allowed in the tournament and if the score was tied at the end of the game, they would have to go through the dreaded 'shoot out.' Five players would be chosen from each team to take a penalty kick in turn against the opposing goalie. If there wasn't a winner after that, two more player from each team would shoot it out and then one player from each team, and that would go on until one scored and the other didn't. It was your basic, soccer horror story.

Chris intercepted a pass from one of the opposition and started up the field. He could hear the cheering and could see two boys between him and the goal, and there was one behind closing in on him. Could he get a shot away? He had to try. He kicked towards the corner of the goal lifting the ball to clear the goalie's head and saw, as it sailed slowly through the air, that the ball wasn't moving fast enough and would be an easy catch for the goalie. But one of his players was streaking by and jumped and smashed the ball down and to the far right. The goalie who was moving to the left didn't have a chance. The ball was in!

Fans were screaming and his teammate turned round to face him. It was Thomas! Thomas had headed the ball into the net and scored his first goal of the season, and it was the winner. They ran towards each other and Thomas gave him an over the head, two-handed, high-five.

"Thanks, man," Thomas said, beaming, "thanks, man."

"Epic goal," said Chris, as happy as if he had scored it himself. "Good for you."

As they walked back to center field to start the play again, teammates slapped Thomas on the back and a couple of them actually high-fived Chris as well. "Good play!" "Awesome!"

He couldn't stop grinning. Finally he was accepted. Maybe it was going to be a good soccer season after all. And just as he thought that, he heard Jaylon yell out, " Go Vikings!"

Oh, yeah. Can't keep the Viking Club down.

THE END

Don't Miss the First Viking Club Mystery!

Written and Illustrated by Maureen Grenier

SOMETHING'S MISSING

**A missing father ...
A missing team ...
A missing friend ...
What more could happen?
Oh, no, something else is missing!**

Three young hockey players struggle with something missing in their lives as they and their teammates play in the annual Vikings versus Pirates Tournament. As well as being anxious to help wrest the trophy from their archrivals by winning first place in their respective age groups, the three Vikings have other worries.

Chris is mourning his absent father, desperate for his dad's encouragement since there is never any from his coach; Jaylon can't seem to forget his former winning team, and knows he is now a loser on a team that can't seem to catch a break (and probably can't help win the trophy); and Rebecca is devastated when her best friend betrays her. But a father, a winning team, and a friend aren't all that's missing. Something else has disappeared and if it's not returned, fingers will be pointing at the whole Viking organization!

Chance draws Chris, Jaylon, and Rebecca together as the last game of the tournament is played. Can they head off the disaster facing the Vikings and the whole town? The three friends put their own problems behind them and concentrate on trying to solve the mystery before the tournament ends.

*Order it from Amazon in paperback or Kindle version,
or from Barnes and Noble and independent bookstores.*

ABOUT THE AUTHOR

Maureen Grenier has worked as an artist for The Kanata Standard, an editor and writer for Meridian Magazine, Publications Manager for the Canadian Institute of Actuaries, and freelance editor and writer for various organizations and publications. She has a BA from the University of Waterloo, a year of Commercial Art from Washington State University, and an Elementary School Teacher's Certificate from the University of Victoria, BC. She wrote and illustrated the first Viking Club Mystery, Something's Missing, in 2012. For more information about Maureen, please visit her website at http://maureengrenier.com.

Printed in Canada